HITCHING A RIDE ON CHRISTMAS EVE

& Other Stories

PETER REX

Contents

Introduction

This short story collection has been 35 years in the making. A gentle reader might ask, "What took so long?" The only reply I can provide is, "That's what can happen when a writer doesn't have a deadline."

I wrote my first short story about Christmas in 1987 when I was in college and I continued to write one almost every year until 2015 when I completed *Snow Angels,* which is included in this collection. Each year, I set a strict word limit of 2,000 words for the story because that's typically all that would fit on a standard-sized card which I mailed out to friends and family members around the holidays. As I edited these stories over the past several years, I waived my self-imposed word limit, though they all remain short shorts.

For this collection, I have picked 12 stories that are ready to head out to the world and find their way. Thanks to my friends and family for their encouragement over these past 35 years and the deepest thanks to my wife, Ann, for making sure this book crossed the finish line gracefully.

Catapult

(2001)

When I was in college, my friend Jack talked me into building a giant catapult – not one of those middle school science project dowels and rubber band jobs, but one capable of launching a bowling ball 150 feet. When I asked him why he wanted to construct such a thing, Jack said, "Back when the Romans used catapults as weapons, they called them 'onagers' which translates to 'wild ass.' That seems like reason enough to build one, no?"

We spent hours drawing up detailed plans, discussed it with our two favorite physics professors, checked out the engineering lab on campus that would be needed for the construction. We hit an impasse when we began to order materials. I backed out because our vision, which was nothing more than a whim, far exceeded my college student bank account. Now, nearly two decades after that project fell apart, I stood next to Jack, passively fighting over a Radio Flyer wagon under the harsh fluorescent lighting of Toys R Us two days before Christmas.

If it had been 15 years earlier, Jack and I would have had a field day with the scene of two youngish fathers tangling over a toy.

"Hey Pete, look at those two" he would have said in his best William F. Buckley imitation. "Apparently Plato and Xenophon are debating the merits of a toy wagon, another sad ramification of liberalism run amok."

"Jack, if I've said it once, I've said it a million times: true happiness never comes from personal possessions. Happiness can only be found in the bottom of a bottle." Then we'd bust out laughing.

But that was back in college in the 1980s when irony and ridicule were the vernacular of our waking hours, when the idea of having kids was something we'd only consider after we'd earned our first million.

A young employee approached us. Her oversized plum-colored work vest almost perfectly matched the purplish highlights blazing through her blond hair. Her name tag read "Nessie." "Is there something I can help you with?"

"Do you have any more wagons, Nessie?" I asked.

"I'm positive we have none in the back," she said with an air of confidence that you hear occasionally in teenagers who have been put in positions of authority and are eager to show off their expertise. "To be honest, we don't stock many wagons. They take up a ton of room, we don't make much money off them and they're a bitch to assemble, pardon my French."

I had the rightful claim to the Radio Flyer. The number one rule of panic-induced Christmas shopping is that the first customer to pick up a product has claim to it. I'd been there first, and as I inspected the wagon, out of the corner of my eye, I noticed a guy approaching me. He wore a blue cotton sweater with no jacket, despite the robust Wisconsin snowstorm, and when he put two fingers along his lips in what used to be an ironic gesture of contemplation, I realized it was my college buddy, Jack.

"Pete!" he'd said when I looked over at him. He gave me a brief hug.

Here's what you need to know about Jack: he successfully campaigned to have *Let's Get It On* as the theme song for his high school prom because official photos of happy couples always listed the name of the song at the bottom of the prom picture; he lost his mom to lung cancer during his first year of college; he forgave me when I slept with his ex-girlfriend; he loved to flirt with young women and many fell for him. Jack liked to call into sports radio shows imitating an old man with a thick Midwestern accent who insisted that the Green Bay Packer players should always wear a sport coat and tie when they traveled to away games. Then he'd sit back and laugh at the flood of callers who thought professional athletes should be free to wear whatever they wanted.

Jack loved to hold court with a group of friends in a 1980s college version of the Algonquin Round Table and he needed a foil, a role I filled easily. He was a Young Republican Reaganite who had organized a "pro capitalism" rally on May Day of his sophomore year and although intended to be (somewhat) tongue-in-cheek, it led to some media coverage and a job offer from a state senator. I was an idealistic liberal who limited my political activism to campaigning for candidates who never stood a chance of winning. Jack double-majored in business and English while I double-majored in political science and journalism. Jack created mischief like Eddie Haskell and I smoothed out the damage like Wally Cleaver.

"How are you?" I asked. "Who are you shopping for? What's going on?" I had neither seen nor heard from Jack in nearly a decade.

"You'd be proud of me. I've got a three-year-old boy. Ethan. Got married a couple of years ago. The whole catastrophe."

"Same age as my son, Spencer."

"No kidding. That's great. Really great."

The ambient buzz of the overhead lights filled a momentary pause in the out-of-date Christmas retail soundtrack. When we were in college, Jack and I made fun of television shows or movies with a lot of awkward silences. Now, we were having one.

Jack grabbed the handle of the wagon and took it for a slow walk down the aisle, imitating an exhausted, slump-shouldered preschooler. I laughed.

After college, I'd moved out to Seattle where I taught high school social studies. Jack served as legal counsel to the governor of Wisconsin. We kept in touch for a couple of years and he came to visit once, but after awhile, Jack stopped responding to any of my phone calls or emails. I could never figure out why he had ended our friendship.

"Pete, I've done a bad thing," he said as he walked the wagon back to me. It was the standard introduction to our many confessions, some serious, some not.

"Oh yeah? What?"

"I procrastinated again," he said. I shrugged. "But what about you, Pete? Aren't you the responsible type who finishes his shopping by Thanksgiving?"

"Hell, there's no way I was going to haul a wagon on the airplane to Madison. We got in last night. My parents are renting a place out on Lake Mendota. They figured all the grandkids could experience a white Christmas for once."

"You could do a lot worse."

"So you think your son is ready for a wagon?" I asked.

"Yeah, Pete. It's all he wants. This wagon." Jack exhaled a shallow breath, lungs still clogged from years of smoking. "I called around, Pete. Swear to God, all the other stores are sold out."

I wasn't surprised. In the recent blockbuster movie, *Another Toy Story*, the character of Roadie (a Radio Flyer Wagon) rescued Woody, the Tom Hanks character, by weaving perfectly down a big hill while the bad guys who are in pursuit on Razor Scooters crash into a pile of trash cans. Ever since, little red wagons had become precious commodities. Razor Scooter sales had plummeted.

"Three-year-olds don't know what they want," I replied.

"You haven't met my son," Jack said.

I knew a couple of months before Christmas that I was going to buy Spencer a red wagon. It was the perfect antidote to all the plastic junk that littered toy store shelves. The Radio Flyer Little Red Wagon with its removable wood sides was a triumph of nostalgia, transportation and utility all in a neat, road-ready package.

Despite my admiration for the wagon, I wasn't sure whether I wanted to deal with the hassle of getting it back home on the airplane and I knew that Spencer wasn't going to be disappointed if he didn't receive one for Christmas. But I also didn't want to give in to Jack.

"Pete?"

"What?"

"Remember that time we talked about that book?"

In our final year at college, we spent an entire night talking about a single sentence that Jack had found buried in a collection of stories by Sherwood Anderson.

That night 15 years earlier, Jack had started the conversation abruptly, as he often did. "Pete, what do you think he means by the sadness of sophistication?" Whenever we talked, Jack assumed we were always thinking about the same thing so there was no need to provide briefings, transitions or introductions to conversation topics.

"What are you talking about?"

"The scene in *Winesburg, Ohio* where George Willard looks back on his life for the first time, and Anderson writes, "The sadness of sophistication has come to the boy.""

We swatted around a million interpretations. Jack thought it was about rites of passage that turned boys into men and I thought it was more about the knowledge that maturity brings as a person grows older. Even though we were barely older than the 18-year-old character in the story, the conversation felt hopeful and permanent. Now, as a father in his thirties, I knew a lot more about the sadness of sophistication.

"Yeah, I remember that time. Did we even know what the hell we were talking about?" I said.

"It felt like we did."

With that memory and his calculated appeal to our past friendship, I realized that I couldn't take the wagon. But I still didn't want Jack to have it either. It didn't seem fair.

"Do you like being a dad, Pete?"

"Absolutely."

"Me, too. You'd be proud of me. I'm a good dad."

"I have no doubt about that." As I pictured Jack playing with his son, my feelings of competition and anger slowly melted away. I thought whatever barriers had been blocking our friendship might be removed if I let Jack have the wagon.

"You take it," I said. "I'll find something else."

"You were here first. It's only fair."

"I'll let you take it," I insisted. "But you have to tell me something."

Another awkward silence. Jack pulled an "inspected by" sticker off of the wagon. "What is it?" he asked finally.

"What happened? Why did you stop being my friend?"

"I don't know." Jack looked out toward the parking lot.

"Was it because I didn't want to build a catapult?"

"Of course not."

"So what happened?"

Jack picked at the fingernail of his thumb. "I got tired of feeling like you were my dad."

The answer confused and then wounded me, the stab you feel when somebody so close seems to misunderstand you so profoundly that it makes you question whether you even know yourself.

"It wasn't anything you did," he said, "but more just how I felt when I was around you, like I was the irresponsible kid, always guilty, meeting with your disapproval, always screwing up somehow."

"What are you talking about?" I said, a bit too loudly. "You were the successful one. You were the one who got into politics when I wanted to. You were the one who went to law school. You were the one who got the big-shot job after college."

"Yeah, well…"

I waited for him to say something more, a brief admission, an apology or some attempt to resurrect our friendship. Jack took the black handle of the wagon and pulled it down the aisle toward the cashier. The right rear wheel rim was bent out of shape and it wobbled comically.

I considered pointing out the flaw to Jack because he didn't seem to notice it but then figured it was up to him to fix it. As I walked toward the front of the store, I pulled an art set off the shelf and followed behind him.

At the checkout counter, we stood silently, two men with their last-minute gifts. As Nessie scanned the red wagon, the LED readout flashed $39.99. The correct price of the wagon was $79.99. Jack looked at me and raised one eyebrow like he used to back in college when something was amiss. I stared as blankly as I could. He shrugged his shoulders at me as he handed the cashier his credit card. I tried to keep myself from shaking my head, and I think if I did, it was barely noticeable.

As he pulled the wobbly wagon toward the door, Jack paused and looked back at me. "You know that catapult thing would have worked," he said.

"We didn't have the sophistication for that job," I said.

He shrugged. I paid for my art set and walked out with Jack into the blowing snow.

"Jesus, I should have worn a jacket," he said. I didn't say anything. "So Pete, where are you staying?"

"Wind Point Guest House."

"That's a great spot," he said. "We had a fundraiser for the governor out there a couple of years ago."

"Yeah, it's nice."

"I'll try to give you a call this weekend. Maybe we can get our boys together. We'll throw them in the wagon, put on some crash helmets and see how it handles in the snow." He smiled and waved as he walked to his car.

Continental Divide

(2007)

"Thank God you're home," my mother said as my brother Danny strolled through the front door two days before Christmas. "I've been worried sick about you."

Her customary greeting provoked a customary recitation of harrowing stories from the 21-hour drive across the Continental Divide, from Danny's college apartment in Utah to our house in Milwaukee: black ice in Wyoming, a speeding ticket in Nebraska, a swerve and a miss with an opossum in Iowa.

Danny hugged my mom, shook hands with my dad and lifted me up until my head grazed the ceiling of our family room. My brother frequently treated me like I was either five years older or five years younger than my true age of 10. As soon as he set me down, I took his picture with my new Kodak camera. In the photo, the last image I would have of Danny for several years, his typically-natural smile looks forced.

Danny handed me a cassette of his latest blues music favorites. He treasured songs with risqué lyrics and double entendres that always annoyed my mother. "Listen to this one," he said turning up my parents' stereo. Lightnin' Hopkins sang, "I want to play with your poodle. I mean your little poodle dog." My mother's brow furrowed and my brother laughed. He mimicked Elvis singing "Blue Christmas" while mixing himself a whiskey and club soda.

"What's your rig out there?" my dad asked. "Looks like a parade float."

My brother typically ventured home driving his latest reclamation project – a 1962 Austin Healey one year, a 1964 Alfa Romeo the following. Two large Rorschach oil blots on our driveway served as constant reminders of those previous Christmas visits.

"It's a Chrysler New Yorker," he said. "Wanted something a little more stable this time."

As the clock approached midnight, Danny settled into a recliner chair and happily described his skiing adventures, his misguided professors and a blues musician with a pet raccoon on his shoulder who played at the club where he tended bar in Salt Lake City.

•◆•

The next afternoon as we were about to leave for Grandma Mary's house, my dad called out to my brother. "Let's take your car."

"I can't. My stuff is in it."

"So pull out your duffel bag, put it in your bedroom and let's get going. Grandma hates it when we're late."

"Go on ahead. I'll take Squirt and meet you over there," he said, opening the car door. "My car needs gas so I'll be a few minutes behind you and Mom."

Danny tossed a large rectangular box wrapped in newspaper into the back seat. During the half-hour ride to Grandma Mary's house, he monologued about all the teachers I needed to avoid once I reached high school, how to convert my five-speed Schwinn into a mini-bike and why he hated Richard Nixon.

According to our family tradition, we exchanged gifts on Christmas Eve at my grandmother's house, a process we termed the "embarrassment of riches." During a break in the action, my grandmother announced that the boy who used to cut her lawn had been killed in Vietnam. My father looked over at her from across the room. "Say Mary, do you have any more cheese and crackers?"

My grandmother ignored his attempt to distract her. "I think it's just terrible what's happening over there," she said, clutching my mother's arm.

"We need generals who know how to lead and politicians who will let them," my mother replied.

"Mary?"

"Yes, dear?"

"Cheese and crackers?"

"Sure, go ahead and bring some in for us. You know where they are." She turned to my brother. "I'm so happy you're not going there, Daniel. Such a waste. How is college going? Dating any pretty girls?"

"Always," he said. "Always." He stirred his drink with his index finger. My dad looked over at him. Nobody said anything for a minute. My brother fetched the long rectangular box and told me to open it.

I tore at the newspaper wrapping. "An electric football game -- it's just what I wanted!" I said. I hugged my brother.

"It's the Packers vs. the Patriots," he said. "I figured you'd like that."

I stared at the picture on the box of the two teams lined up against each other on the green metal field. I quickly learned that when you lined up all the players in formation, as soon as you turned on the power switch, some of them moved forward while others invariably went around in circles. Some of the players broke free from the line of scrimmage and headed immediately for the sidelines.

My grandmother stood up and gazed out the window. "I sure do like your car, Daniel. Seems more like a car I'd have in my driveway," she said.

"I can let you take it for a test drive some time," my brother said.

"Looks like you have a lot of boxes in there. Are you moving home?"

"No, Grandma. But I'm not going back to school." My parents looked over at him.

My father cleared his throat as he often did before he was about to say something important. "So what are you going to do?" he asked, setting aside his can of Schlitz and plate of Ritz crackers and cheese squares.

"My draft number came up. I got the magic letter from Uncle Sam five days ago."

"You got called?"

"Nixon changed the rules for college deferments a few months ago so I guess they figure I'm fair game."

What I did not realize then is that like hundreds of thousands of other young men, my brother's trajectory had been permanently altered by the draft lottery of December 1, 1969. When I was older, I tried to imagine Danny watching the CBS News Special Report with his friends from college, watching as a bland man in a dark suit opened a little capsule with a piece of paper inside and read off the date, repeating the process 366 times. Within the first few minutes of the draw, Danny's birthday, December 30th, had been chosen, the third highest draft number. I wondered what he had said to his friends and how I would have responded if I had been in my brother's shoes.

My mother looked at my dad and turned to my brother. "My goodness, I had no idea, Danny." She walked over to the couch where my brother was sitting and put her hand on his shoulder. "So how does the car fit into all of this?" my mom asked.

"It's just easier to haul my stuff."

"But you haven't unpacked any of it," she said.

"Mom."

She frowned. "No, no, no." She shook her head. "Daniel James, you know that's not right. That's not honorable. That's not how you were raised."

My dad stared out the window for what seemed like a long time. "Son."

"Dad, I know you were in Korea and I respect you for that," he said. He looked at my mother. "I know all the arguments. I know all I can know about it."

"Your great grandfather fought and died in World War I defending this country," my mother said. She pointed to a picture of my grandfather that sat over the mantle next to an array of medals. "Your grandfather, a teacher, fought and died in World War II defending this country. Your father fought in Korea defending this country. When called, we serve. That's what we do."

My mother neglected to mention her 14 years of service as a U.S. Army nurse, a job she held until the beginning of the Vietnam War when she transitioned to her current position as a school nurse.

"Mom, this is different. I can't go over there and try to kill innocent people. We have no quibble with them."

"You'll go to jail," my mom said. "I can't bear the thought of that."

I stared at the electric football players scattered all over the metal field, frozen in their positions. My grandmother picked imaginary pieces of lint off the arms of her green couch.

"This war is wrong and if it means jail, I guess that's what I'll have to do," he said quietly.

"Good for you," my grandmother said. "You've always carved your own path, Daniel, don't stop now."

"Mother, this is none of your business."

"Lighten up, dear. It's his life."

"Where will you go?" my mother asked.

"He could go to the cabin." My mother looked at my father as though she couldn't believe what she had heard. Our family owned a small cabin in Two Harbors on Lake Superior near the Minnesota-Canada border. For three weeks every summer we called it home. Apart from that, it was empty. "You could stay at least through the winter."

"Howard, I can't believe you're encouraging this."

"Margaret." He looked down at his shoes and shook his head. "It's…there's no sense in the terrible things I witnessed."

"I know that but you survived it. You went because it was your duty."

He reached for her hands. "I know it looks like I survived it. I did. But for the past 15 years, every time I read the morning paper, all I see is cruelty. Men killing other men. Every time there's a loud noise…"

"Think down the road, Howard. How will he find a job? He'll always be looking over his shoulder, saddled with guilt." She straightened out a wrinkle on her skirt. "Danny, of course I'm worried about you."

"I know."

"But I can't lie for you."

"Mom, I would never ask you to lie." He forced a smile. "Just don't turn me in."

Perhaps she knew better than the rest of us what his decision would mean, not only for my brother but for me, for her and for my father. "I can't promise that either."

It is the most brutal thing I have ever heard my mother say and for a long time, it made me question my love for her. But now, after many years, I wonder whether she wanted to make sure she didn't know where Danny was, so if anybody ever came looking for him, she could respond honestly.

"Margaret, you should be ashamed of yourself," my grandmother said. She stood up and walked briskly into the kitchen. A minute later, my mother grabbed some empty glasses and followed Grandma Mary out of the living room. I heard their voices talking over each other while dishes clanked in the kitchen sink.

At the end of the evening, I figured out that wherever Danny was headed, he was leaving immediately. The five of us stood in the driveway. Cold, damp air filled the night.

"I've loved being your grandma and will be praying for you, Danny. Don't drink too much, don't do drugs and stay out of trouble," she said. My brother looked amused at Grandma Mary's warnings as he hugged her. He promised her that this was not the last Christmas they would celebrate together. Then he turned to me.

"I'd like to say I'll keep in touch but it might be awhile," Danny said. I nodded. "This is what it feels like to lose a brother," I thought. I turned away and pretended to inspect his car.

My mother took Danny's hands in hers and looked him in the eye. "Be safe." She let his hands go, complained about the cold evening and walked back into Grandma Mary's house. Grandma followed her.

My father hugged Danny. "I might be able to find a doctor who could, you know, cook up something to get you out of this."

My older brother, the toughest person I knew, held on to my father. When Danny let go, his eyes were watery. "Thanks, Dad, but I can't."

⚫◆⚫

Two years later, my parents and I were sitting down to Christmas dinner when we heard a loud car downshifting as it rounded the curve toward the house. My heart raced a bit as it always did when I heard the rumble of a sports car. Two yellowish headlights reflected on the ice covering our driveway. A car door slammed. I listened for a familiar voice to be singing "Blue Christmas." My father got up immediately. A look of hope erased the wrinkles that had formed around his eyes.

Tommy Rutkowski, Danny's oldest friend, stood at the door.

"I'm just stopping by to wish you a Merry Christmas," he said. "I brought you a fruitcake. You were always the only ones who would buy a fruitcake from me when I had to sell them for our high school band."

"We always hated those, Tommy. I thought you knew that," my dad said.

"I suspected, but I was never sure," he said, handing the fruitcake to me. "What are you hearing from Danny? Last I heard, sounded like he was maybe headed to boot camp."

I wondered whether my brother had changed his mind and decided to go to Vietnam. It seemed unlike him, but as I got older, I understood the power that mothers have over their sons. Maybe he was over there and didn't want to give us the satisfaction of knowing that he was more scared to not fight than to fight.

"I'm afraid he's not going to make it home this Christmas," my dad said.

"I knew it was a shot in the dark," Tommy said. "Next time you talk to him, tell him to give me a call. I'd love to get caught up with him. Been too long."

"It has," my dad said.

❧

Two years later, after the Vietnam War had ended, the secretary at my high school walked into my biology classroom and handed me a small package. There was no return address but the postmark stamp read Toronto. As I opened it, a cassette tape, a photo and a brief note fell out.

"Remember what I told you -- stay away from Mr. Killinger and Mr. Losey. You won't learn anything from those jokers. Here's some music I think you'll like. Love, Danny." In the photo, my brother leaned against a small black sports car. His hair was shorter than the Christmas picture I had taken of him four years earlier. His facial expression, which in his college days often had a fox guarding the hen-house quality, now looked more cautious, more restrained.

I smiled and burst into laughter. "Is there something you'd like to share with the class?" asked Mr. Killinger. I shook my head.

When I got home, I gave my mom a long hug.

"What's that for?" she asked. I handed her the package.

She sat down on the couch, stared at the picture and note and then closed her eyes for a full minute before handing it back to me.

"Put the tape on the stereo," she said. "Let's hear those awful songs."

Family Tree

(1995)

Juliet snapped off the kitchen radio like she often did, silencing the voice that had frustrated her for so long. She poured three fingers of cranberry-infused vodka into a tumbler, added three ice cubes and sat down in a bentwood chair at her kitchen table. For a minute, Juliet thought about letting it go. She looked at the telephone sitting under a canopy of *The New York Times* and a stack of student essays that were awaiting her red ink.

Juliet dialed the number and it connected to a taped promo: "KFRE – speaking the truth about freedom – it's Marty-In-The-Mid-Day." A snippet of Muzak droned in her ear briefly (Juliet recognized the tune as a wordless version of Poison's "Every Rose Has Its Thorn") and then she was on the air as Marty-In-The-Mid-Day said, "Juliet from Forest Grove, go ahead."

"Umm, hi Marty." Juliet realized that her voice echoed throughout the empty two-bedroom house. She'd never noticed, or maybe she had forgotten, the way the sound bounced off the walls when she talked.

"Hi Juliet. Thanks for calling and welcome to the show. What's up?" he asked, all sunshine and warmth.

What was up was that she could no longer stand listening to his conservative bullshit. She wanted to ask: "How can you view the world this way, Marty?" but instead she said, "I'm calling regarding your comments about allowing Christmas celebrations in public schools." She knew the radio host recognized her voice.

"Great. What's on your mind?" he asked.

How many hours had she spent listening to Marty and his familiar phrases, his familiar thoughts, anticipating exactly what he was going to say? She found his predictability both comforting and irritating, like a scar she couldn't stop touching.

"I celebrate Christmas, but I think that we should respect the rights of people who aren't Christians," Juliet said.

Marty responded calmly. "Listen, I never said that other kids should be forced to participate in Christmas concerts or events. I'm only saying that it's natural for kids to get in the holiday spirit at home and at school. What's so bad about putting up a Christmas tree in the school cafeteria? Students who don't like Christmas trees can just ignore it."

The host's practiced tone reminded Juliet of the time her boyfriend had proposed to her in a redwood forest in Northern California, reciting a cheesy monologue that he must have contemplated for weeks. "Redwoods are like love, they keep growing forever until nothing but a lightning strike or human intervention can harm them. Look at them, Juliet," he said, caressing her back. "These huge trees start from tiny saplings and they grow more magnificent and filled with life as they age. Redwoods symbolize love, like the love I have for you."

In retrospect, the redwoods had come to strike her as stubborn symbols of inflexibility.

"So Juliet, what's wrong with having our kids sing 'Silent Night' in music class?" asked Marty-In-The-Mid-Day.

She stumbled back into the conversation. "For most of us, there's nothing wrong with singing Christmas carols. But kids shouldn't be required to celebrate a God they don't believe in. I've heard you say that governments make it their business to stick their noses into our business. And now you're encouraging churches to stick their noses into our schools."

"See Juliet, you haven't been listening." God how she hated his smugness. "The Forest Grove School Board members are the ones who issued a policy prohibiting Christmas celebrations. They stuck their collective noses into *our* business."

She remained silent for a minute, recalling her admirer's marriage proposal. At twenty-four years old, Juliet had been susceptible to the idea of being in love. She embraced its aura, its taste, its geometry and vocabulary. Her mother had warned Juliet that women should never marry before they're thirty, and even though she adored her mother, she adored the idea of being in love even more.

Juliet had started to say "yes" to her boyfriend's proposal, but he had continued on and on, stating all the reasons why they should be married, as if he were arguing a case before the Supreme Court. She had nearly walked away.

The radio host pounced on the dead air before listeners could switch the station.

"Juliet, do you have any kids in school?"

"*Damn you*," she thought to herself.

"Juliet?"

"Yes, I have a daughter in fifth grade."

"And are you looking forward to spending some time with her during Christmas vacation, or 'Winter Break' as the Forest Grove School District calls it?"

"Of course I am."

"So what's the big deal? You think it's okay for your daughter to have a week of Christmas vacation approved by the school district, but you're opposed to kids singing a few Christmas songs in class?"

"*Why are you so hung up on Christmas carols,*" she thought. What she said was, "This country has always respected the rights of people who don't agree with the majority and I'd hate to see us forget that."

"I can't argue with you there. Have a great afternoon, Juliet. Call me again some time."

Juliet looked at the huge weeping willow in her back yard as she hung up the phone. She stared at it, slumped in her chair and thought back to the time in the redwoods. Her boyfriend's marriage proposal ended only when she had gently placed her index finger over his lips, and whispered, "Yes, Paul Michael Martin, I will marry you."

Wedding. Job. House. Child. Routine. Juliet turned the calendar faithfully each month, barely noticing the words that she had scrawled in its tiny boxes: "Baby class." "Alison to Pre-School." "P.T.A. meeting." "Sacred Heart Church picnic." "Soccer practice."

Juliet looked over at the radio, recalling Marty's last-minute accommodation. He had actually admitted, "I can't argue with you." And then the polite sign-off. The gall! Juliet finished the glass of vodka as soon as she heard a car honk in the driveway and she smiled as her daughter, Alison, walked through the front door, clad in her soccer uniform.

"Hi Mom! How was teaching today?"

"Fine. Come here for a minute, I want to show you something."

Alison immediately spotted the Christmas tree that her mother had purchased and set up in their tiny family room. It had taken her nearly an hour to wrestle it properly into the stand.

"Mom, you bought a tree! Can we invite Dad to come over and help us decorate it?"

Juliet gazed with admiration at her daughter's expectant eyes. "He'll probably have his own tree at his apartment and I'll bet he's going to need your help decorating it before you go to church on Christmas Eve." Alison frowned at her mother.

For the first few years of marriage, Juliet and her husband saw the world similarly. They agreed that life was confusing, chaotic, exciting and absurd and every day, they celebrated that truth. And then as one year replaced another, Juliet and her husband's discussions became filled with static as they disagreed about politics, their jobs, culture, child rearing, religion. Tones of voice shifted. Simple questions led to endless debates and raised voices.

"Why can't we fight about money or duties around the house like every other married couple?" Juliet complained one night. "Why do we always have to have these deep philosophical arguments about the war in Bosnia or whether the *New York Times* should have published the Unabomber's manifesto?"

"What are you afraid of, Juliet?" he said. "Why can't we talk about things that are important?"

"We're not really talking. I say something and you tell me why I'm wrong. That's not a conversation."

"So maybe you should come up with some different ideas," her husband said.

"You know, I just came up with one," Juliet replied. She closed her eyes and resolved to be a different person, one who would never again be dependent on another human for her happiness.

"Mom?"

"What?"

"Can we invite Dad over this weekend?"

Juliet stared at the tree, noticing that despite her best efforts at centering it in the stand, it still leaned to one side.

"Did you call him?"

"We talked today."

After their final argument, Juliet had decided that love with her husband wasn't a redwood, it was a Christmas tree that she had dressed up in garland and lights and ornaments and stuck in a stand in the middle of her house to admire for a short period of time.

Their divorce had been amicable but it left Juliet with the seemingly permanent feeling that love was fleeting and tenuous, filled with misperceptions both intentional and unintentional.

"You called him on his radio show, didn't you?"

The way her daughter emphasized the words "didn't you" made her sound so much older than her 10 years.

"Yes, I called him during his show."

"Did you ask him if he could come over to decorate the tree?"

"We didn't really talk about it."

"Why not?"

"It wasn't the first thing on my mind."

"Maybe you could call him tomorrow and invite him over."

"I don't know, Allie."

"Remember when we used to pick out a Christmas tree at Stewart's Farm and you and Dad never agreed on what kind to get? That was funny, wasn't it?" Alison smiled faintly at her mother, waiting, hoping for affirmation.

"Was it funny? I don't know, it didn't seem like it." Juliet regretted the remark when she saw Alison's shoulders slump. Her daughter looked away as she walked over to the Christmas tree. Alison reached up to see if she could touch the top of the tree, falling short by about a foot. She leaned into it and took a deep breath, soaking in its competing residues of nostalgia and pine. "This tree is exquisite."

Juliet had never heard her daughter use the word "exquisite" before. It sounded beautiful in her young voice. She had no idea that Alison would get so excited over a misshapen $30 scotch pine. Juliet watched her daughter tug at a branch to see if she could pry a needle free. She reached in to feel the bark of the trunk and then frowned when sap stuck to her fingers. The sight of her daughter discovering the complexity of the tree comforted Juliet, making it seem possible to create something lasting from something temporary.

Alison finally turned around and met her mother's stare. "What?"

"Nothing. I just…nothing."

Alison said, "I think Dad should see this. He likes to decorate trees and he always knows right where to put all the ornaments. Besides, we need somebody tall to put the star on top because I can't reach it. We can listen to Christmas carols while we decorate the tree, just like we used to. Can we call him? Please? Can we?"

Juliet walked over to the kitchen radio, grabbed a paper towel and wiped off a years-old gravy stain that had been stuck to the grooves of the speaker. She flicked on the radio and turned the dial until it landed on KSNO, a station that played nothing but holiday music for the month leading up to Christmas. She didn't recognize the song that was playing, something about the singer not wanting any presents or toys for Christmas, all she wanted was to keep waiting under the mistletoe.

"I like this song," Allison said. "It's really popular right now."

"I don't know this one," Juliet said as she walked into her bedroom, opened a closet door and pulled a box of ornaments from the top shelf.

Girl in the Toll Booth

(1999)

"Why is it that every time you come to see me, you try to change me?" she asked. "You're my brother. You should know better."

"I know that working as a parking garage attendant isn't your calling," I said. "My God, look at this place. You're the last person in Seattle who gets paid to breathe in car fumes."

On Christmas Eve, my sister Sarah sat in a five-foot by four-foot Plexiglass toll booth waiting to collect money from last-minute downtown shoppers, all for $9.50 an hour. For three years, she had floated from job to job, intellectually slumming on her master's degree in education.

Sarah stared straight ahead as she leaned out, arms resting on the aluminum frame of the half door, chin resting on her hands. On top of the cash register, a copy of *The Winter of Our Discontent* sat like a ragged tent over the LED readout tower of the till. Just to the left of the doorknob were three deep dents, like somebody had tried to hammer their way into the cashier's booth. The garage reeked of exhaust.

My sister turned away to look for something in the booth and emerged with a copy of the *Seattle Times*. "Look at this," she said, opening the newspaper. "This woman refuses to sell her house to make way for a new 12-story condo development. That's who I want to be, the person who won't move to make way for another goddamn computerized parking lot and pre-paid spaces." I laughed. I loved her like any brother loves his hopeless sister which meant that I didn't have the heart to tell her the world would not bend to her will. "Seriously, do you know how many people have lost their jobs because of this so-called high-tech boom?" she asked.

"About a tenth as many as those who have found jobs," I said.

"You would know," she said. Sarah often teased me about my job as an editor for SweetHomes.com, a website that featured flattering "reviews" of high-end houses throughout the Pacific Northwest. In truth, the homeowners paid for the articles as a precursor to listing their expensive houses for sale.

"C'mon," I pleaded. "Please?" More newspaper reading. "I didn't drive all the way here to watch you read the newspaper."

"Why exactly *did* you come here, Darren? Did Mom and Dad tell you to do this? Are they cutting me out of their will unless I shape up?" My sister made her fingers into air quotes as she said the words "shape up." "That would be so typical of them."

My parents used to joke that they spent $100,000 so that a small liberal arts college in Oregon could radicalize my sister against capitalism, but they simply had not been paying attention. Throughout her youth, my sister aggressively shared her toys with all of her friends and if any of them showed a modest interest in one of her possessions, Sarah always said, "You can have it."

"First of all, Mom and Dad are not headed for the grave any time soon, and no, they have not cut you out of the will – at least as far as I know. Second, they know better than to send me on a humanitarian mission."

"So, you think I'm some kind of tragic victim in need of your generosity?"

I knew that my sister had recently broken up with her latest girl-friend and didn't have plans for the holidays. Sarah didn't own a car so I hoped to repair this broken familial bond by showing up at her work and bringing her home to spend Christmas with me, my wife, Claire, and ten-month-old daughter, Lily.

"Jesus, why do you have to be so difficult?" I asked her.

"Wait a minute. You come barreling up here and ask me to leave my job in the middle of Christmas Eve? How am *I* being difficult?"

"It's past nine, just leave the gate open. You'll be thumbing your nose at corporate America. That should appeal to you," I said.

"Darren, listen. This is hard for me to say because you're my only brother." She reached for my hands through the rectangular opening of the booth and gave them a little squeeze. "I'm in a different place right now. I'm not into the whole Pottery Barn Christmas nightmare. The big house with innocuous but tasteful looking knick-knacks and all that. It's poison to me. I know your home is probably all decked out for the holi-days, but I just can't. It's cool that you're into it, but it's just not my thing."

"So ignore the decorations. Come see Lily," I begged. "She's almost walking on her own." No reply. "Why are you even working then if money is so poisonous?"

"I follow the Hippocratic Oath. First, do no harm. This is the clos-est I can get. Think about it -- I sell time. What could be more harmless than that?" my sister said.

"More like wasting time. Why would anyone want to spend their Christmas Eve in this hell hole?" I said. I worried that Sarah's philo-sophical purity would relegate her to the fringes of society, financially and socially.

"That's so like you. Totally judgmental. Everybody should want what you want, right?" She rubbed her eyes. "I do this job because it helps pay my bills. I'm not stupid. I realize I need food and shelter."

"Whatever happened to becoming a teacher so you could help students see the world as it really is?" I asked.

"As I've told you many times, teaching isn't confined to classrooms," she replied.

"Agreed. But I'm not seeing many learning opportunities inside this dump unless you're teaching your friends how to put on bullet proof clothing. I read there was a shooting just down the street from here last weekend."

"This is my life, Darren. I'm sorry that you don't approve of it."

I ignored my sister. "Let me paint a picture for you. We drive home tonight, talk about old times, like when we heard sleigh bells on Christmas Eve as we fell asleep. Remember that?"

"I do," she said, a big smile revealing what was left of her adolescent dimples. For a moment, it felt as though I'd broken through. "You're very sentimental, Darren."

She was right. I felt nostalgic for all of our holiday childhood routines. When we were young, Sarah and I pretended to be characters from *Lost in Space*. We'd imagine we were marooned on a distant planet and desperately tried to make it home for Christmas. A few years later, we loudly practiced off-key duets of classic carols and threatened to sing like that in church and then laughed when my mother said she'd cut off our allowance for two weeks if we did.

"You can help me set out some presents. You'll sleep like a log. In the morning we'll have a huge breakfast, anything you want. I bought lots of vegan options for you. Then we'll take a walk around the neighborhood with the barnacle child -- that's what we call Lily because she clings to us like a barnacle. Later we'll call Mom and Dad and wish them a Merry Christmas. Then we'll stoke up the fire and you'll open your presents."

"You got me presents?" she asked, her voice breaking out of the weary monotone that I'd become accustomed to hearing.

"Yep. And they're good." We'd bought Sarah a gray pearl earring for her pierced left eyebrow and a signed copy of *Manufacturing Consent*, a Noam Chomsky book that she had raved about a few years earlier.

"Really? What are they?" she asked. "Give me a hint."

"They're a surprise. But I promise you'll like them."

"That's kind of you." She took a deep breath. "I appreciate the invite, but I've really been looking forward to having a low-key day tomorrow, you know?"

As I looked at my sister, it felt like we were no longer related. Our portrait of shared experiences seemed to be fading, like passing a highway billboard that becomes clearer and clearer as you approach and then it's behind you and all you have are memories of what it looked like for that brief moment before you sped past.

"Give me three reasons why you won't come home."

"I already gave you my reasons."

"What can I do to change your mind? I'll drive you back tomorrow, no problem."

"Darren, you can be really irritating. Do you ever listen to yourself? Cajoling, arguing, selling, every minute, non-stop. You're like an annoying television commercial."

This was always the point we reached, every time we spoke for the past year or two. An utter dead end. I couldn't remember the last time we'd had a nice conversation. "Sarah, what's happened? Really. Please. Just tell me what I did." She looked down at her newspaper. A police siren blared off in the distance. "Please."

Sarah set her newspaper aside and looked directly at me. "It's not anything you did. It's that you won't acknowledge my world. You always want me to be part of your world rather than understanding mine."

"What does that even mean?"

"It means I don't live in a *sweet home*, I live in a cramped apartment because I don't have any money and I have to live very simply, but you wouldn't know that because in the 18 months I've been here, you've never once been to my apartment. You're an hour away and you always invite me to come to Olympia. Whenever you come to Seattle, you insist on meeting me for coffee or you want to try some new restaurant that I can't afford. Why do you do that?"

"I don't know. I guess I never realized I was doing that. I'm sorry."

"Time to make amends. I'll close up a bit early here and you can come to my apartment and have some tea."

"I hate tea," I said.

"Let me paint a picture for you. We'll talk about old times, we'll look out the window and watch cars pass by and we'll make up stories about who's in the cars and where they're going. I'll turn on the radiator full blast. The place will get so warm that you'll fall asleep on the couch just after you admit that the tea wasn't so bad."

"Do you still have that crappy green corduroy couch that Mom and Dad gave you?"

"Of course."

"I do love that couch."

"Then in the morning, Mr. Davis from across the hall will shuffle over and knock on the door. He'll ask me to pick up a couple of things at the store because he's nearly blind and doesn't like to go out on cold mornings, and he'll give me some money but it won't be enough because he hasn't shopped for himself for five years and still has the old prices stuck in his head. I'll wander down to the 7-11 and get him some squishy white bread. Margarine in a tub. Canned tuna. And when I get back I'll give him fourteen cents in change even though I had to dig into my own pocket for the final dollar."

A red Toyota Camry with significant body damage on the driver's side passenger door pulled up to the toll booth. The driver handed her ticket to my sister with a $10 bill. In the back seat, two toddlers tussled over a package in a Target shopping bag. My sister scanned the ticket, gave the driver her change and wished her a Merry Christmas.

"So, what's your plan?" Sarah asked after the Camry was out of the garage.

"I can't miss Christmas with my family."

"I thought I was part of your family."

"You're making this difficult for me," I said.

"You're the one who drove up here out of the blue."

"It's our first Christmas with Lily."

"She's a baby, she won't even remember it. But you'll remember how we hung out on Christmas Eve."

"You know I can't do it. I can't just abandon Claire. Why does it have to be tonight?"

She sighed. "Everything involves sacrifice, Darren. I'm asking you to make a sacrifice for once. That's the toll. That's how much it costs."

The smell of exhaust made me queasy. I couldn't understand why my sister had drawn this line.

"Too high," I said. I looked down at my hiking boots and when I looked back I noticed that Sarah was reading her newspaper again. "But let's do it next week. I'll come check out your place and we'll spend the whole day together. I'll bring your presents."

"Sure, next weekend." Her tone of voice mystified me. I couldn't tell whether she was being sarcastic, agreeable or something else.

"I gotta go. It'll be almost midnight before I get back home."

"Right."

"Are you going to be around next weekend?" I asked.

"Probably. Maybe. I don't know."

"I'll call you," I said. She shrugged and then nodded her head a couple of times. "Bye, Sarah. I love you. Merry Christmas."

"Say hi to your family."

I walked down one level of the parking ramp to my car and pulled around to Sarah's toll booth. I handed her the ticket that I'd received upon entering the ramp. "You can have this back," I said.

My sister took the ticket and inserted it into the slot of the cash register. "That'll be four dollars and fifty cents," she said, sticking her hand out.

I smiled. She looked back at me with what I thought was a look of contentment. "Really? You're kidding, right?"

Sarah said nothing. A second passed, then another, another, another, another, another. She shook her head and exhaled.

"Darren." She looked at me, impassive, flicking the switch to raise the gate. "Just go."

Hitching a Ride on Christmas Eve
(1996)

I stepped into the dingy bathroom of Room 107 at the Snore and Whisper Motel. The toilet seat slipped off its hinges as I lifted it to pee. "What a dump," I said.

"What else is new?" Dawn said. She pressed her foot down on a ripped crease in the green shag carpeting. "It's humiliating."

My nine-year-old stepson, Sam, slid a Monopoly game out of his backpack (found recently in a free box at a garage sale) and set up the board on one of the marshmallow-soft Queen-sized beds. Charlie, who is seven, claimed the metallic car as he always does.

We played Monopoly for a couple of hours, laughing and enjoying ourselves, a better way to pass the time than sitting in front of the idiot box. Eventually, I started to rake in big money and there were fewer smiles as I prepared to bankrupt my wife and stepsons. Sam had only a handful of bills left when he landed on my prime hotel property, Marvin Gardens. "Come to Papa," I said.

"Don't be such an ass," Dawn said. "This is already a terrible Christmas Eve. Don't make it any worse."

Dawn told me many times she had no regrets about our situation, but I know the truth.

Every day we hitch rides. I'll pick a destination an hour or two away which gives me time to talk good-hearted drivers out of some money, usually enough for a cheap motel room or a meal before we go to a shelter. People tell me I have the gift of gab. When a car with a metal fish on the trunk picks us up, I quote the Bible. I know thousands of country songs and keep up-to-date on sports, whatever makes people feel comfortable. Sometimes I'll be honest and tell the drivers that the only way we can survive is on the generosity of people who pick us up. Many nights we end up with nothing.

"Rats!" Sam said, looking at the red hotel I'd placed on Marvin Gardens.

The boys love Monopoly. Sam makes everyone pay their rent whenever they land on his property, no deals. Charlie's got a generous heart. When any of us ends up on one of his squares, he'll say, "That's okay, you don't have to pay me." He always loses. I worry that he'll get burned by people when he's older.

When Dawn gets sick of it, I tell her that Monopoly is good for the boys, shows them it's normal to travel around and stay at motels. When you spend your life on the road begging for money, you look for anything that your kids might understand, even if the main lesson is that life is kind only to those with money.

I closed my eyes and visualized the next day's ride. I pictured a youngish high school teacher in a blue Honda SUV on his way to Christmas dinner at his parents. He'll ask if we hitchhike often and I'll tell him about how after I graduated from junior college, I wanted to check out Mexico, but I was broke, so I jumped trains to get there. I'll point to Dawn and the kids and tell how I met them a few years earlier at a food bank. I'll describe how we caught a ride to Reno, got hitched and just kept on going. He'll ask me about work and I'll tell him that Dawn used to clean houses until her body broke down. I'll talk about the nine months I moved boxes at United Parcel Service and how we rented an apartment. I'll admit that I got laid off after Christmas and after a few months of looking for work, we couldn't afford rent and decided to head back out on the road. I'll brag about how we've seen 29 states and he will nod but won't say anything.

Sam tugged at my flannel shirt and I opened my eyes. His cute face and wispy hair reminded me of a koala bear. "How much do I owe you?"

Part of me wanted to let Sam off the hook. Another part felt that the boys needed to learn about the world. Bills have to be paid. Nobody bails you out. And then a third voice asked, "Why do you make my kids play Monopoly? It just messes them up."

A semi-truck roared by the motel interrupting the sound of *"It's a Wonderful Life,"* which blared from a television set in a room next to ours. It was already past seven o'clock and I didn't have any presents for Dawn and the boys. If we had stayed in one place for a few days, I could have gone to the Salvation Army and picked out some toys for the kids.

I glanced down at the four twenty-dollar bills in my front pocket, my emergency stash. I had stolen things before and knew that I would do it again if necessary, even if it is wrong.

I looked at the deed to Marvin Gardens. Sam asked me again how much he owed. I knew that if I let Sam stay in the game, he'd figure out that I had bent the rules. I thought about taking his railroads and other properties in a trade but figured if he's going to lose anyway, I'd just be delaying the inevitable. Plus, I still wanted to find a way to procure some Christmas presents before it was too late.

Dawn looked over at me like she wanted to help, like she's about to tell me what to do, but then she appeared to catch herself and she waited to find out exactly what kind of man she had married.

Tomorrow, about half an hour into our journey, after the boys have fallen asleep on their mother's shoulders, I will tell the Honda driver about the Monopoly game and will say, "It's moments like that when you need to figure out what you're trying to teach your kids. All I know is there's not much truth in the world. Look at Christmas. We sit around honoring a man with a beard who was born from a virgin while another man with a beard delivers toys to a billion kids in one night."

Tomorrow, Dawn will frown at me from the backseat, breaking her silence and jeopardizing our chance at getting some decent money out of the driver. "The truth is that Santa protects the dream that wishes can come true and Jesus protects the dreams of immortality," she will say.

"But that's not truth," I'll respond. "The truth is that sometimes life isn't fair. Sometimes you get laid off. Sometimes you dream about owning a house and you get stuck renting, or worse, begging for money. Sometimes you lose in Monopoly. There are the lucky few and the rest of us." The driver will not say a word.

Back at the game, I picked up the deed to Marvin Gardens. Just as I was about to tell Sam how much money he owed, Dawn said, "One time I played Monopoly with three hippies. None of them bought any property. They just went around and around the board. All they wanted to do was use their $200 allowance to travel and pay cheap rent. It went on *forever*."

"What does that have to do with anything?" I replied. She gazed at me, waiting for some recognition.

"How much do I owe you?" Sam asked.

"When can we start opening presents?" Charlie asked.

My wife and stepsons stared at me, waiting for answers. I lost track of the questions. I listened to the television set next door, which now emitted moaning and groaning sounds. I felt paralyzed. Words, explanations, answers all eluded me.

"Charlie, can I have some money?" Sam asked.

"You've got enough."

"Not enough to pay Dad. Please?"

"I might need this money," Charlie said, greedy for once.

"It's Christmas goddammit, no fighting!" I said, my head pounding.

Sam said, "We're not fighting. I'm just asking him to help me out."

The three words -- help me out – felt like a slap in the face. Lots of times at the end of the ride when I'm hitting up drivers for money, I'll use those words to close the deal. Hearing Sam use the magic phrase was too much.

I stood up to get a glass of water and as I walked back to the game, I noticed Sam sneaking a few $50 bills from the bank. I looked over at Dawn and she glared back at me, lips pursed.

"Hey!" I yelled, as though disciplining a dog. Sam dropped the bills back into their place and looked down at the board. He threw his small pile of money next to my stack of bills and stomped into the bathroom, slamming the door behind him. The sound of sniffles penetrated the thin walls.

Tomorrow, when my family and I are crammed into the Honda, I will tell the driver how at that moment, I felt like a total loser. I'll tell him that some day when he is a father, I wish that he will never catch his son cheating at Monopoly or anything else. The driver will offer consoling words, saying it's not a big deal, but I will know the truth.

I grabbed the game board, folded up the money and stuffed it into the box. Sam came out of the bathroom, eyes red, and looked at the game without comment. "So, what are we going to do now?" Dawn asked.

"We're going to have a Christmas Eve feast," I announced. We headed out for dinner, walking nearly a mile until we found an inexpensive diner. The lights inside the restaurant were so bright that I couldn't help but stare at the pores on Dawn's face. She looked pale and fatigued, as if all affection had been drained from her body.

"You know our tradition – no opening presents until Christmas Day, right?"

The boys smiled and nodded.

Tomorrow, I will tell the story to the Honda driver and make this admission: "There's no way I can teach my sons any lessons by playing Monopoly. In fact, I'm wondering whether I can teach them any lessons." The Honda driver will reply, "Of course you can." As we approach our destination, I will ask him for a favor. I'll ask him if he could take this vintage version of Monopoly off of our hands. The Honda driver will pause momentarily. Perhaps he'll wonder whether it's all a big story, because after all, I'll have already confessed that we scratch out a life by begging our rides for money. Perhaps he'll figure out that I'm sick of carrying the game around in our backpacks because it doesn't really fit. After a brief hesitation, the Honda driver will offer me fifty dollars which I will spend on presents. Later on, he'll feel a quiet pride as he recalls the story to his parents over Christmas dinner.

The driver will drop us off on a street with a string of motels and he'll wish us good luck. All four of us will watch and wave as the car pulls away. We'll freeze momentarily as the brake lights go on and all of us will wonder whether the Honda driver has stopped and is looking back at us through his rear-view mirror as we walk away from the motels.

I Think I Won

(1998)

Our reclusive neighbor, Charlie Weiss, sat in our living room waiting for me to open a toy I did not want and, as I learned later, he intended to tell the world about it.

Neither my parents nor I knew much about Mr. Weiss because he rarely ventured outside, but here is what I had observed with my ten-year-old eyes: Saluted rather than waved. Drove a gray 1970 Cadillac Eldorado. Always wore solid color polo shirts, black pants, white socks and black shoes. Handed out licorice every Halloween. Rarely mowed his lawn.

Mr. Weiss was recently widowed, which is why my parents had invited him to Christmas Eve dinner, despite limited interactions with him during the past couple of years.

Mr. Weiss arrived at our doorstep with two poorly wrapped presents and what appeared to be a small briefcase. After introductions and small talk, we migrated to the living room for gift opening. Mr. Weiss handed me a long box and I had removed half of the wrapping paper from his present when he stood up and excused himself. We heard what sounded like a briefcase opening and then the distinct tapping of a typewriter rattled out from the family room. My parents looked at each other. My younger sister, Katie, looked at me. An ember from a piece of wood burning in the fireplace popped and flew into the protective screen.

I sighed with an exaggerated air of aggrievement.

"What's up, honey?" my mom asked.

"It's an electric football game. I wanted hockey."

I had asked Santa, my parents and any other potential benefactors for a National Hockey League game, a small-scale foosball knock-off where players pushed, pulled and twisted skinny levers to manipulate plastic skaters.

"How in God's name was our hermit neighbor supposed to know that?" my mother whisper-yelled. Then came her stock phrase: "Let's not get too emotionally attached to inanimate objects." I pouted.

The two games were fundamentally different. The hockey players moved in graceful lines; the electric football players inevitably twirled in crazy circles like a kindergartener who has just stepped off a merry-go-round. The hockey players could be maneuvered skillfully; the football players were ineducable. The quarterback was supposed to "throw" a tiny felt ball, which you had to wedge on his plastic arm and then launch hopelessly toward another player. The football, which resembled a piece of white belly button lint, inevitably ended up lost on the carpet where it would later fall victim to a vacuum cleaner.

"Listen, Mr. Weiss was very generous to bring presents when he barely knows you kids," she said. "When he comes back, I expect you to open that gift and be grateful, goddammit."

Mr. Weiss, a former minister, returned just in time to hear my mother take the Lord's name in vain. He arched an eyebrow. "Sorry for the interruption. Where were we?"

"What were you doing in there?" my sister asked.

"Working on a project," he replied.

"I hope you're not revealing all of our family secrets," said my father. He smiled at our neighbor.

"I wasn't planning on it but let's see how things go," Mr. Weiss said.

Nobody said anything. I finished opening the electric football game and thanked Mr. Weiss as enthusiastically as I could. While I was examining the game, he left us again. My mother went into the kitchen to work on the dinner.

I followed Mr. Weiss into our family room and watched as he sat down at an electric Smith Corona typewriter that he'd brought to our house. He rolled a long sheet of white paper into the jaws of the small machine and tapped at the keys.

"What are you writing?" I blurted out.

"My diary. I'm writing the world's longest, most complete diary. I don't leave anything out. For posterity."

"Cool," I said.

My mother stopped mashing the potatoes and looked over at our neighbor. "How... interesting," she said. "So why don't you just write it when you get home at the end of the night?"

"I can't do that. I'd get too far behind. I have to type every 30 minutes or else I won't be able to catch up."

"Cool," I said.

During our dinner, as soon as Charlie Weiss finished delivering a prayer, my parents interrogated him about his diary.

With the exception of the time he spent sleeping, he divided it into five minute segments, recording everything in short sentences. Mr. Weiss told us that he included the exact minute when he peed. He included his dental x-rays, store receipts and his toenail clippings. When he got his hair cut, he'd glue a few gray strands into his diary.

"How long have you been doing this?" Katie asked.

"I started writing the diary after I retired from the ministry seven years ago," Mr. Weiss said. "I don't know why I started to be honest.

Just looking for something to do, I guess. Once I started writing, I kept going and then couldn't stop."

"What did you do during your wife's funeral?" I asked.

"Peter, that's rude," my sister said.

"It's fine," Mr. Weiss said. "As you can imagine, that was a terribly difficult day. I took extensive notes during the funeral and then typed them up later. I figured I owed it to Mrs. Weiss to keep going."

"Have you ever tried to take a break from it?" my dad asked.

"Nope. I wouldn't know what to do with myself if I didn't have the diary," he replied. "It would be like turning off my life."

I wondered whether Mr. Weiss meant he would die if he stopped writing in his journal but I knew my parents wouldn't like if I asked him that question so I kept it to myself.

After dinner while Mr. Weiss was typing up his latest entry, my parents handed me a long rectangular box wrapped in shiny green paper. Hockey! I quickly assembled the game shoving the Philadelphia Flyers and the Montreal Canadiens players haphazardly onto their aluminum support brackets.

"Does anybody want to play?" I asked as I placed the game on our kitchen table.

"You got a mouth guard, son?" Mr. Weiss asked.

"Why?"

"I knocked out more than a few teeth in our church hockey league and want to make sure you're protected," he said with a chuckle. I looked around for my dad or sister to intervene but it was too late – the challenge had been issued.

We sat down to do battle. Charlie immediately figured out how to score. He'd pass the small plastic puck to his player in the center of the board and give it a quick flick of the wrist.

We played for what seemed like a long time, trading goals and laughing at missed shots. The former man-of-the-cloth did not hesitate to run up the score on me. Once or twice, Mr. Weiss glanced over at his typewriter. After awhile, he got up and walked over to it.

"No, we have to keep playing," I pleaded.

"Hold your donkeys," he said. "I just need a few minutes."

I dropped the puck for an imaginary face off, manipulated my players back into position and slammed home a shot against Charlie's defenseless goalie.

"Ha! I just took the lead."

Mr. Weiss looked at me for what seemed like a long time, though I didn't really think about it until several years later.

I realized that most of the conversation about the diary had been focused on how, when and what but nobody had asked him the most important question. "Mr. Weiss?"

"Yes, son?"

"Why do you keep writing all the time?"

He stared at the hockey game for a second and then asked me to get him a glass of water. After I handed him the glass, I noticed that he didn't type anything.

"I must confess I don't know why I do it exactly," he said finally. "I think I keep writing because it helps me focus on the present rather than dwelling on what I've lost."

I shrugged. "But *this* is the present," I said. I put the puck back on center ice and slammed home another goal.

"That's it," he said hustling back to the game. "I'll take you down faster than Jesus wiped out those money changers!"

"You couldn't even if you tried," I said.

Charlie's players skated ferociously as he moved the thin metal levers like they were extensions of his fingers. The evening melted away, interrupted only by my mom.

"Peter, you better not be awake when Santa arrives. And Mr. Weiss probably needs a break."

"You're right. I need to get ready for Santa myself," he said. He flicked one more goal into my net, stood up and formally shook my hand. "You're a tough player. But I think I won." Charlie packed up his typewriter while I packed up my hockey game.

After that Christmas Eve, Charlie occasionally wandered over to our house to say hello. We'd play hockey or watch an inning or two of a baseball game on television. Sometimes I'd help him with yard work or shovel snow from his driveway. Every Christmas, my parents invited Mr. Weiss for dinner but he never accepted because he had started a new tradition of spending the holidays with his sister and her family.

When I went to college at the University of Wisconsin several years later, I lost touch with our old neighbor. One day, my mom sent me a month-old *Milwaukee Journal* newspaper obituary about Mr. Weiss with an attached note: "Thought you would want to know about Charlie."

In part the obit read, "An avid diarist, Mr. Weiss set out to write the world's longest journal in 1967. The diaries, which take up 74 archive boxes, are now part of a local history collection at the State Historical Society at the University of Wisconsin."

A couple of days later, I walked to the Historical Society library to read a small portion of Charlie's diary. Most of the entries were pretty bizarre. "11:00-11:05: Drank six ounces of milk. Opened seven pieces of mail. Utility bill, $28.25. 11:05 – 11:10: Read article in TIME magazine about Watergate."

I asked for the box that contained our Christmas Eve dinner. As usual, Charlie had divided the day into brief periods. "7:35-7:40: Drank eight ounces of decaffeinated coffee and ate one piece of apple pie. Cleared six glasses and five plates and placed them in the kitchen sink. 7:40-7:45: Conversed with Rex family about their plans for Christmas Day. They will attend morning mass at Sacred Heart church and have dinner with their cousins."

The next entry was short and direct. "7:45-8:30: Played NHL hockey game with neighbor, Peter Rex." That's all it said.

I turned the page and looked for more words about our game or the rest of his evening. The next entry was headlined only, "Christmas Day, 1974." The passage told generally about his day, without the five minute increments. I paged through the rest of the typewritten sheets in the binder and found that after that evening, Charlie had abandoned his all-inclusive approach in favor of a more traditional diary. The entries focused mainly on his thoughts and feelings. "Spent a few minutes discussing politics with Elmer. He thinks Ford did the right thing by pardoning Nixon. I'm not so sure that Nixon should be forgiven until he asks for forgiveness."

Charlie even skipped a few days in his log. After our Christmas Eve hockey game, the journal entries, and their author, had changed.

I sat and read the diaries for a couple of hours until the library closed. I packed them up and placed them carefully into their boxes. As I walked to my apartment, I broke down in tears, not because Charlie had died but because of the apparent loss of what had defined several years of his life, the goal of writing the most complete diary in history.

I called my mother and told her how reading Charlie's diaries had left me devastated.

"Oh honey, you're looking at it all wrong," she said. "That journal was an unhealthy obsession for Charlie. He didn't realize that it was totally keeping him from sharing his life with other people. I think it was his clumsy way of trying to distract himself after he retired and his wife died."

"But his diary was important to him," I said.

"Listen, as long as he had that journal, Charlie wasn't living. He couldn't travel. He barely left his house. He was oblivious to everything but that damned book. You were too young to notice but it was very disconcerting to watch a person lose himself like that."

"I know that playing hockey with Charlie didn't change his mind about the diary but something happened that night," I said.

"You're right, something did happen. I'm not sure what it was but we do know that he started to have more of a life. You gave Charlie a gift and thank God for that," she said.

A couple of months later, I discovered my old hockey game in our basement and gave it to Gordie, a 10-year-old boy who lived across the street from my parents. I showed him how to play and ran up the score on him.

Misfit Toys

(2008)

Like most older writers, my father would love to reclaim a handful of characters from his famous stories, fix their blemishes, polish them up and send them back out into the world. This is the story of how I set out to do exactly that for him as a Christmas gift.

Act One: During a Christmas visit to see my parents, my two little boys and I cuddled up to watch *Rudolph the Red-Nosed Reindeer*. My father wandered in and sat down on the leather couch to watch a few minutes of the show. During an early scene when Rudolph and the other young calves are practicing their flying, his fake black nose falls off, revealing its true color. All are horrified. Santa says, "Donner, I'm ashamed of you," (presumably for siring a red-nosed reindeer). Comet, the alpha male coach, mocks Rudolph and encourages his pupils to reject their compatriot.

My dad shook his head. "I always hated that part. Santa is too one dimensional. He comes across as an intolerant bastard. Criticizing Donner? It's too much!"

"Grandpa, why are you so mad about this show?" asked my six-year-old son, Spencer.

He ignored the question like he often does. "I tried to shave off his crankiness in the final draft, but the producers insisted that Santa and the reindeer shun Rudolph because that's how the original poem and song went. That always bugged me."

I agreed. The scene had serious flaws. When I was in college, my buddies and I would disparage people who had wronged us by saying, "we won't let him join in any reindeer games, will we?" Reciting one of the most mean-spirited lines in the history of children's television programming always struck us as hilarious so we often repeated it.

Buying a present for my father is impossible because he has no material needs. He made a nice living at a time when we rewarded creative people with rich imaginations. He and my mom live in a beautiful condo in Florida overlooking the Gulf of Mexico, he plays golf whenever he wants, drinks nice vodka, and his wife, three children and nine grandchildren all adore him. On that night as we sat by the television, I decided if there was something in *Rudolph the Red-Nosed Reindeer* that always bugged my father, I would attempt to fix it as my gift to him.

Over the following months, I hatched a plan to fly to Los Angeles and pitch CBS into revising the harsh scene into something more palatable. I'll admit, altering a long-running and beloved television show sounds far-fetched, but three factors worked in my favor to secure a meeting with a key network official. At the time, my sister-in-law, Erin, was an executive for CBS in charge of all of their digital content. She worked down the hall from the Vice President for Programming at the network. Second, television loves to honor their own, even an obscure writer from the 1960s like my father. Finally, CBS had been working to digitally remaster *Rudolph*, preparing him for his debut in High Definition. Every now and then, television producers will make small variations to shows when they remaster them, changes which then get teased out to entertainment reporters to gin up media interest in old chestnuts like *Rudolph.*

◆

Act Two: My wife, Ann, hated the whole idea because she thought I was putting her sister in a difficult spot after Erin had worked so hard to move up the corporate hierarchy at CBS. After arguing about the scheme for a few days, she made her final proposal: "For all the money you're spending on this harebrained plan, we could have a computer geek just edit a DVD of the show and give that to your father," she said. "I'm willing to pay for that."

"It's not the same," I said.

"I guess I find your fondness for grand gestures charming when it involves me and irritating when it involves others," she replied. I knew not to say another word and hoped it was the end of the discussion. After nearly an hour of silence, Ann reluctantly handed over our one remaining credit card, the one that we had not cut up in a naïve and unsuccessful attempt to reduce our debt. I quickly booked the flight to Los Angeles.

As Ann drove me to the airport to catch my plane for the meeting at CBS, I felt a kinship to the pariah reindeer who had foolishly headed out into the snowy wild to look for his family when he finds they've left home to look for him. The only difference between us was rather than a red-nosed reindeer heading off into a deadly blizzard and ill-fated conflict with the Abominable Snow Monster of the North, I, a human man, was flying to meet with a television studio executive in the drought-stained sprawl of Culver City, California. As she stopped the car in the airport departure lane, Ann looked me square in the eye: "Please don't do any serious damage while you're there." Like Rudolph, I trudged on.

Prior to the meeting in Los Angeles, I had only read about people who spend $400 for a haircut. When I met Tristan Scott, I realized I was in the presence of such a person. My sister-in-law introduced me to the thirtyish CBS executive with hipster black frame glasses, perfectly-managed coal-black hair and a pressed French blue shirt.

"So you're Roger's son. He was a giant in this industry for a long time," said Tristan as he greeted me with a smile and gentle handshake. I kept myself from laughing out loud at the use of the word "giant." For six years from 1962 until 1968, my father was the head writer for Rankin/Bass, a television production company specializing in animated holiday specials. He wrote the teleplay for *Rudolph,* creating characters like Hermey the Dentist, prospector Yukon Cornelius and Clarice, the oddly attractive love interest/doe. My father also wrote the script for *Frosty the Snowman* and several lesser-known shows. Eventually he left television to work as an advertising copy writer because it had, in his words, "better pay, better clothes and better liquor."

"Tell me, Peter, what's your father up to?" Tristan asked. I'm usually put off by faux familiarity in which the speaker frequently drops a person's name into the conversation, especially when that individual is almost young enough to be my son, but I shrugged it off and replied that he was well. We made small talk. He offered me some green tea and complimented my sister-in-law for her brilliance. I admired the view of the San Fernando Valley from his office. All seemed to be going well.

"I'm here because I understand you're in the process of remastering *Rudolph the Red-Nosed Reindeer.*"

"One of our subsidiaries is doing that work," he said, nodding.

"I think you should make a minor change to the show."

"Really? Like what?" I noticed the hint of smirk on his face.

"Tristan, I'm so sorry," said my sister-in-law. "I thought this was just a meet and greet." She looked at me and for the first time, I noticed wrinkles in her forehead. I could see Erin's carefully constructed move up the studio ladder starting to wobble because of me.

"It's fine. Let's hear the pitch," Tristan said.

I described the offending scene. "My father believes that Santa and Comet need to be softened. It would only take a couple of small changes to make it less malicious."

58

Tristan laughed. "You're serious?" At this moment, I realized I was putting Erin's job in jeopardy. I envisioned her being called in to a meeting of fellow executives where she would have to defend me for having the gall to suggest fiddling with a Christmas television classic. And yet, at that moment even though I knew I'd made a terrible mistake, I was unwilling to extricate myself gracefully. I bulled ahead, ready to endure a lifetime of in-law tension or mockery.

"I have two suggestions. They're easy edits."

Tristan put up his hand. "You know the show is based on the song. *'All of the other reindeer, used to laugh and call him names…'* "

"I understand that but my thought was after Rudolph's fake nose pops off, Santa wouldn't need to say anything, he could just shake his head in disappointment. That would make him seem less severe. And Comet could say, 'C'mon all of you, let's go,' and lead the other reindeer off-screen rather than announce that Rudolph wouldn't be allowed to play any reindeer games. Viewers would still feel his isolation, but it would be less cruel than currently depicted."

"You know that this is the longest running Christmas special on television."

"I've read that."

"I'll be candid with you. It's awfully difficult to change a show that so many people know so well. We have millions of viewers who have memorized every line of *Rudolph* and if we changed it, we'd hear from them."

"You think viewers would be upset if you made Santa less inconsiderate? Or Comet less callous? It could open up a whole national dialogue about harassment and bullying. It'll boost ratings."

Tristan sighed. Erin stared at my forehead, trying to bore a hole in my skull with her eyes. "You know that neither you nor your family have any legal claim on this."

"Of course. I'm just here to pitch you an idea. Nothing more."

"And it's a very interesting idea, Peter. I'll give it some thought," he said, rising from his chair. "Please say hello to your father for me."

◆

Act Three: There were 14 of us gathered around my parents' table for Christmas dinner later that year for the traditional meal of filet mignon. Every year right after saying grace, my dad recites the same line: "Everybody needs a little red meat at Christmas."

As soon as he had delivered his signature remark, I jumped in. "Dad, I know you've asked us to not buy you anything for Christmas so I just have a story to share." I told him about my efforts to transform *Rudolph* into something closer to his original vision.

"Oh, that was never going to work," he boomed, taking a generous sip of his martini. "I could've told you that. Number one rule of the networks: never touch a cash cow, you might sour the milk! But God love ya' for tryin.' You are top shelf son, top shelf."

"I tried to tell him many times it wouldn't work," said Ann.

"I thought it was worth a try," I said.

"Course you did, you're my son! *Charge of the Light Brigade* and all that. Great story. Can't wait to tell it to some of my buddies out at the golf club."

I had heard my father use this tone with me many times in my adulthood, an inflection that seemed to say, "I raised a son to conquer the world, not tinker with it." He looked at me across the table and could tell that I felt hurt.

"Hey c'mon now. You think I'm yanking your chain. I'm not." He put down his fork and rubbed his hands together.

"Listen, here's a story that I've never told you. *Rudolph* premiered in 1964. It was one of the first shows I'd ever written that actually made it on the air. So you and your mother and I stretched out on that ugly plaid couch to watch our little black and white television. Your sister was still a baby so I think she was sleeping and your brother wasn't born yet. We're watching the show and your mom is trying to find ways to compliment me. It's not exactly *To Kill a Mockingbird,* if you know what I mean, but she did her best to find the highlights." He winked at her.

"After the show was over, you gazed at me and asked with this sad little voice why Rudolph never kept his promise and made Santa stop at the Island of Misfit Toys. You were the most innocent and sensitive five-year-old boy on earth and you were right on the mark — it was this glaring oversight. I don't know how I missed it. Looking back on the original version of the show, Santa comes off like a total jerk — he never came back for the Misfit Toys! So the next day, I confronted Jules and Arthur and told them we had to change the ending because it was going to sink the show and leave kids with a bad taste. They were reluctant to change anything because they're Jules Bass and Arthur Rankin Jr. and they thought their scat didn't stink."

"What's scat?" asked my five-year-old, Ben. My father chuckled and resumed his story.

"At the time, I was three months into the teleplay for *Frosty the Snowman* and I point blank threatened them. Told them I would walk and take my script with me unless we changed the ending to *Rudolph.* Well, they couldn't look like they had made a mistake so they cooked up this whole story about kids waging a letter-writing campaign about the ending and how that drove them to change it."

My father looked directly at me. "Here's the truth, son. We added that ending because of you. So now during the closing, Santa comes to the Island of Misfit Toys and puts them in the sleigh and delivers them to houses. It added humanity to the show, thank God, because without it, *Rudolph* would have disappeared off the map after 1965 and your mother and I wouldn't be living in this house. If you're ever writing a Christmas story, it's gotta have a heart. Hear me?"

I shook my head. "You're making all this up. I don't remember saying anything like that to you."

"Of course you don't remember it, you were five years old! Look it up on the internet. You'll see I'm telling the truth." My mother smiled at me but didn't say anything.

My son Ben looked over at his Grandpa and then at me. "You did that, Dad?"

"You bet he did," my father replied, pointing a piece of steak on the end of his fork at Ben for emphasis. "And don't you ever forget it."

Price of A Gift

(2006)

"I need you to help me steal eight hundred bucks from Willingham," Nick said to his roommate.

"The econ professor?"

"Yeah."

"Isn't that, like, unethical?" Trumain knew his college buddy loved to cook up cloak-and-dagger projects, but they'd never run afoul of the law.

"Hardly," Nick replied. He leaned forward in one of the two canvas lawn chairs that constituted the bulk of their living room furniture and then looked behind him, as if they were not the only ones in the drafty duplex. "Listen, every semester Willingham teaches Intro to Macro to 400 students and he forces them to buy this piece-of-shit $150 textbook that he wrote *ten years ago* just so he can pocket the royalties. He creates his own little controlled economy and then lectures about the infallibility of the free market system. Hypocrites deserve to have karma bite them in the ass."

"I thought karma is when fate intervenes, not when a student decides to steal from you."

"Screw off. It's a victimless crime. End of story."

Trumain laughed. "I must have skipped that chapter in the law books I've been reading."

As Christmas approached, Nick felt the pressure to buy the right gift, more so than any other year and it had left him feeling clumsy and desperate.

"What's the money for?" Trumain asked him.

"I'm getting Lilly a pair of diamond earrings."

"South African bling-bling? For that chick? Hell, she must have drawers filled with jewels that her daddy bought for her."

"Why do you say that?"

"You told me her family was loaded. I heard she had never brushed her own hair before she came here to college."

"For your information, her old man died last year and even though he had some cash, he never spent it on his kids. And Lilly would never buy them herself."

"Okay but still, diamond earrings? Man, you must be into her."

"I'm in love," Nick said.

"And this time, I mean it," they said in unison. Both laughed.

"Seriously. She's super smart. Beautiful. Funny as hell. Confident. She's got it all."

"You go for that brunette, no make-up thing?" Trumain asked.

"This time I did."

"Are you two even going out officially? You haven't slept with her, right?"

"No and no. That's why I really need a breakthrough. I'm treading water."

"No offense, my man, but I think she's out of your league."

"What do you mean?" he asked, but he already knew what his roommate was about to say. Nick had always considered himself as firmly in the middle class, making his way through a public university with a combination of student loans, occasional checks from home and money from his job on campus. Nick assumed that with hard work and a little luck, he would eventually find his way to a higher social circle, but lately, he had started to question that belief.

"You're playing double-A ball and she's playing for the Yankees," Trumain said. "She's a philosophy major! Only potheads and trust funders end up with a degree in philosophy and she ain't no burnout. You work for university food service and constantly reek like a deep fryer. Plus you're a grad student in *journalism*."

"I thought you liked covert projects."

"Of course I do, as long as they're legit." Trumain shook his head and looked at the carpet. "I'm pre-law, man. You know what I got riding on this." Trumain, the first in his family to go to college, felt more pressure than pride on his shoulders. He knew that he was expected to graduate with honors, go to law school and provide for his parents and older siblings.

"Have you ever read *Gift of the Magi*?" Nick asked.

"Where the dude buys his wife expensive brushes but she's chopped off her hair and sold it to buy him a fancy watch?"

"Yeah, that's the one. I read it again the other day and it finally struck me that it's not a lesson about generosity or personal sacrifice. The lesson is don't be a chump. Don't give away the thing that makes you unique to show your love for another."

"You think *Gift of the Magi* is a call to thievery?" Trumain asked. "Jesus, you are one messed up pony."

"Please?"

"Why don't you just work some extra hours at the Snack Shed?"

Nick paused. "That'll take too much time. Christmas is just around the corner."

"It's only mid-November."

"Listen, I've already made up my mind. Your role is minimal, but I need your help, Tru. Please?"

Trumain walked into the kitchen, muttering to himself about the prospect of getting caught and booted out of school while he grabbed two beers and a half-eaten bag of potato chips. For four years, he'd watched every one of his roommate's crushes emerge and fade as his romantic schemes crumbled. He knew Nick's latest idea would end badly but Trumain valued their friendship as it was one of the few he had maintained during his entire time as an undergrad.

Nick laid out the plan. It involved memorizing the professor's credit card number when he came through the line at the university cafeteria, a jewelry store in Chicago that took phone orders and a UPS delivery to the professor's house while he was hopefully away for Thanksgiving.

●◆●

Three weeks later, Trumain sat on the floor of the duplex, reading a criminal law textbook and making notes on index cards. His roommate came in just before midnight. Nick tossed his jacket onto the lawn chair and walked toward his bedroom.

"Hold it there, man. Come on back and lay it down. Full disclosure like you promised."

Nick turned, sat down on the floor, slouched against the wall and kicked off his shoes. "What are you working on?"

"My criminal law final's tomorrow. Enough stalling. Tell me what happened."

"We went out for dinner to celebrate our last final. Drank some beer. Laughed a ton. Everything was perfect except in my mind I had imagined that it would be snowing everywhere and we'd sled down Jefferson Hill but then this fog rolled in and messed up the whole winter postcard thing."

"Damn global warming. There's never a good snowstorm when you need it."

"No doubt. But at least the fog made everything quiet. Nobody was around. It felt like nuclear war was imminent and we were the last to know. So we're walking to the top of Jefferson Hill and I wanted to do something spontaneous so I coaxed her to sit with me in Abe Lincoln's lap."

"You climbed onto the Abe statue? The pedestal alone is six feet high."

"Tell me about it. So we scramble our way up there and the fog is everywhere and it's totally beautiful."

"Until…"

"Until we're sitting there making small talk and she can tell I'm nervous and so she's getting nervous. In the middle of a sentence, I interrupted her and said, 'Hey. I love you.'" For once in Nick's life, he felt like he had sounded right when he said it. His voice wasn't shaky or quiet or jokey or uncertain.

"Did she freak out on you?"

"Nope, not at all," Nick said.

"Hell, she's probably had dozens of guys profess their love for her. She's probably got her reaction down pat. A whole routine."

"Screw you."

"Continue."

"So I get the jewelry box out of my pocket and hand it to her before the moment gets too awkward. And I said, 'I got you a Christmas present.'"

"How original."

"I know, a firm grasp of the obvious but it was all I could manage."

"Did she like those shiny little rocks?"

"I'm getting to that. So she opens the box and when she sees the diamonds, her brow furrowed for a second like it took a moment to register. Then she lights up. "Nicholas! Oh my God, these are incredible.

They're so beautiful. Where did you ever?' She stops herself, drapes her arms around me in this awkward hug because we're sitting on the statue, but she gives it a try and then she says, 'Thank you. They're the nicest gift I've ever received.'"

"Did you lock lips?"

"Briefly. She nuzzled into my neck a couple of times and we kissed for a minute. Then she pulled back, took a deep breath and patted her chest a few times, you know that gesture people make when they're pretending to have a heart attack? She does one of those."

"Dude, no, not that gesture. It's like when a movie star wins some hokey award and they do that. People should only use that gesture ironically or if they're actually having a heart attack."

"Exactly. So we jump down off Abe and she pulls out her earrings and puts in the diamond studs and turns to ask me how they look. I'm raving as much as I can for a piece of jewelry, telling her how beautiful she looks and she gives me another big hug."

"Sounds promising."

"I thought so, too. So I whisper in her ear one more time. "I love you.""

"Hang on, I think I need to get a beer to hear this next part."

"Grab me one, too." Trumain grabbed four bottles of Miller High Life, opened one for Nick and set the second bottle on the carpet next to his roommate. "And one to grow on."

Nick took a deep breath, rubbed his eyes and raised his beer bottle in a silent toast.

"So you put it out there again? Man, you are a bold puppy," Trumain said.

"I don't know what I was thinking. She pulls back and looks me square in the eye and then she hugs me again so we're cheek to cheek. And then she says it in this quiet, kind voice."

"What?"

"I know you do."

Trumain shrieked. "What? Let me get this right. You say, 'I love you,' and she says, "I know you do."

"Exactly. But I'm trying not to look upset or anything which is nearly impossible because she's looking me in the eyes, I mean she's just locked and I kept my gaze as long as I could but then I couldn't anymore and then I finally looked down at the ground."

"Whoa. That ain't right, forcing eye contact after she's leveled you. That's unnecessary roughness!"

"It was brutal, man. What can I tell you?" Nick exhaled again and took a long swig from his beer. "Maybe she's just not ready to say it back yet. Sometimes it takes time for a person to get caught up."

"Dude, anything's possible. But it seems like she's not feeling it."

"Yeah, I know," Nick said. He shook his head. The evening had left him with a bruising epiphany about unrequited love: Lilly completely understood him, his feelings and motivations, enjoyed the glow of his affection and still was not moved to fall in love with him.

"I was able to keep it together for the walk home but that was it. Kissed her goodnight and left her at her loft."

"Did she invite you in?"

"Negative."

"Did she give you a present?"

"No. I don't really want anything."

"Man, that is one sad sack tale. You must mean a lot to her, but sometimes it just ain't enough, is it?"

Nick shrugged. "I guess not."

"Hey, one more thing."

"Shoot."

"I don't mean to get all Moral Majority on you but I gotta know. Was it worth it?"

Nick carefully peeled the High Life label off of his beer bottle. He thought about Christmas, about what people give and what people get, and how until this year, he'd been able to navigate the tension between the material and the spiritual, and find joy in the generous intentions of others. Finally, Nick looked back at Trumain. "That was a nice thing you did for me, helping with the earrings. I love you, man."

"I know you do."

"Screw you!"

Ruth Willingham sat on a mid-century couch by the fireplace, watching the flames dance among the embers of the spent birch logs. She sifted through a large pile of Christmas mail addressed to her and her husband. After she read nearly a dozen cards and tossed the junk mail into the fire, she opened the Visa credit card bill. The professor's wife skimmed the charges, smiled happily and stuffed the bill into her purse, hiding it until after Christmas.

Snow Angels

(2015)

When people ask me if I like Christmas, I always lie and say, "Of course. Who doesn't like Christmas?" But most often, it reminds me of what I did to my brother, C.J., when I was 16 years old.

My parents had left me to take care of my younger brother so they could finish their last-minute shopping and preparations for Christmas Eve dinner. Outside, clumpy Milwaukee snowflakes parachuted down, casting a ghostly light on the fading afternoon. C.J. eagerly wanted to be a part of the storm so I dressed him in his puffy turquoise jacket, high-tech gloves, neon hat, snow pants and boots. He waddled out the door, seemingly bulletproof, and motioned for me to join him.

As I put on my own winter gear, my phone buzzed and like all addicted teenagers, I picked it up. I felt the flutter when I saw the text was from Holly, a years-long crush. I met Holly in our seventh grade English class and immediately became infatuated when I overheard her at lunch one day performing a spot-on imitation of Miss O'Flaherty, our teacher who had a thick Irish accent. Our friendship picked up steam at the Friday night middle school dances where we regularly battled each other in ping-pong (she flirtatiously claimed to know *all* my tricks) and we cracked up other students with our off-key versions of "Heart and

Soul" on the surplus piano that they hauled out for such events. Then there was the time Holly and I nearly drowned in a canoe because we were laughing so hard when it began to take on water and sink in slow motion. As our middle school careers turned to high school, I quickly learned that our time together was inversely proportional to Holly's contentment with her lackluster series of boyfriends. Nonetheless, her message arrived like an unexpected Christmas present.

Holly: Making my list and checking it twice. Have you been naughty or nice?

Me: Ummm.

Holly: I have my answer!

Me: Do you know where I keep my Christmas stocking?

Holly: LOL! My parole officer says I'm not allowed to break into houses to deliver presents.

C.J. knocked on the window and waved for me to come out. I nodded and resumed my texting with Holly. At the time, it didn't seem like I had neglected my younger brother for very long but when I looked outside into the growing darkness, I couldn't see him. I told Holly I needed to run, dressed quickly and went to look for C.J.

Although my brother is quite independent in many respects, our family rule is that he isn't to be left unsupervised for more than a few minutes. As a socially active teenager with two working parents, this obligation to keep watch over my brother often felt like an overwhelming and unfair burden.

I called for C.J., looking for a turquoise blob against the gray palette. As I hustled down the driveway, I noticed the shape of a snow angel in our yard and another one in our neighbor's yard across the street, and at the next house as well. I ran up the street and one block over, following my brother's trail of innocent snow art, his Christmas gift to all of our closest neighbors. Then I saw the terrible scene.

Laying on the ground next to an idling car, C.J. writhed in agony, his right foot turned at a traumatic angle. As I approached, I heard him say, "Matty left me, Matty left me."

Prior to that moment, my brother may have been one of the most beautiful 13-year-olds on the planet. It was as though the DNA gods had worked themselves to exhaustion creating his blue eyes, high cheekbones, curly blond hair and his perfect muscles, pores and bones – until they got to the part where they wired up his brain and added the magic neurotransmitter chemicals, a job they carried out in a way that left C.J. different from other kids.

An old woman huddled over my brother. I recognized her as Mrs. Castor, the retired lunch lady with bug-eye glasses who walked her dog incessantly and drove an ancient Ford sedan.

"I didn't see him," she said. "I don't know why he was laying so close to my driveway. He should have known better."

I put my hand gently on my brother's chest. "I'm here, C.J. Everything's going to be okay."

"It hurts, Matty. It hurts."

"I know, buddy, and I'm going to take care of you." His body remained stuck in his final snow angel mold.

"Make it stop hurting, Matty."

I turned to Mrs. Castor. "Please call 911. My parents aren't home right now and we can't wait."

"I don't know what he was doing so close to my driveway," she repeated. "You should have been watching him."

"Please. Can't you see my brother is in pain?"

"I just got home from church – otherwise I wouldn't be driving in these conditions. Those children's choir masses always run long when everybody just wants to get home."

"I'll keep that in mind but we need to take care of my brother. Can you please call 911?"

She looked sadly at C.J. "Oh yes, dear. Of course. I'll run right in."

A few minutes later, C.J. and I sat wedged into the back of an ambulance on a dark journey that I would re-live for the next decade. As I stared at my brother, sitting on a stretcher and surrounded by intimidating medical paraphernalia, I thought about his pain and the inevitable doctors' appointments and parental interrogation. I realized that this Christmas weekend, and other weekends, were ruined.

After that night, I made many futile efforts to apologize to my brother. I tried random gifts, public apologies at family events, notes of regret taped to a huge tub of licorice, all unacknowledged. Eventually, my father put a stop to it.

"Why don't you realize it's about atoning, not apologizing," he said. "C.J. doesn't do apologies."

Over the next few years, I made amends to my brother, one deed at a time. We shared a handful of dinners at Tubby's Burgers, his favorite restaurant. I invited C.J. to stay with me for a weekend in my dorm at college and introduced him to all of my friends. I really hit the jackpot when I bought my brother a pair of tickets to "Legends on Ice," a diverse troupe of skaters who performed routines with one less twist, Lutz or toe loop than their Olympics programs to adoring audiences. I gave C.J. the tickets for his birthday in September and he obsessively e-mailed me about it for months.

My brother and I had a history with ice skating. Every winter, when the Whitnall Park pond froze, we'd lace up the skates, grab a couple of sticks and play an admittedly rudimentary game of hockey. One time when he was nine or ten, C.J. body-checked me into a nearby snowbank and I landed with a loud "oof." The novelty of the moment and my involuntary exhalation delighted my brother, so every time we played hockey at the park, he would crash into me and wait for me to fall.

A few months after the Christmas accident when C.J. had completed all his rehab, I stuffed a pillow under my jacket as an extra layer of protection and we trudged out on the pond to re-create his triumphant body check.

We put on our skates and glided tentatively onto the ice. A minute later, my brother collapsed on his bum ankle. He looked up at me in tears. "It hurts, Matty. I can't skate." I thought we might need to tighten his laces or maybe wait a few weeks or allow another four seasons to pass but we never did make it back out on the pond together.

My actions on that Christmas Eve and my efforts to make amends to my brother changed me. I became exceedingly cautious, fearing that any inattentive moment could potentially bring pain to others around me. This restraint left me feeling out of place when I started college at the University of Wisconsin-Madison, a trait that Holly often noticed and commented upon from the comfort of her dorm room at Northwestern. Whenever I told her I was hunkered down studying, she inevitably messaged me: "When are you going to do something fun and start acting like a real college student?"

In addition to prodding me to take more chances, Holly regularly mocked our risk-averse culture. She decorated her room with stolen caution signs that graphically depicted the worst-case scenario of the hazard – like a car getting pelted with rocks in an avalanche warning sign or a person getting zapped by a high-power line.

One day during our sophomore year, I texted her a photo of a caution sign of a stick figure getting swamped by a huge wave and Holly replied immediately with three selfies.

In the first photo, Holly mimicked the silhouetted figure in the high surf warning sign, arms akimbo against an imaginary wave, her face frozen in mock horror.

In the second, she held up a note. "Wanted to buy: cheap teleporter."

In the third, she looked straight into the camera with an uncertain smile and held a piece of paper reading, "I've been thinking about you a lot lately."

I nearly passed out. Unlike the stacks of romantic signs I'd misread for the previous seven years, this one seemed promising.

I texted her: Are you coming home for Christmas?

Holly: Yes! Only for one night. My family is headed to Cabo on Dec. 22. Let's get together and go out on the 21st. Can't wait to see you!

Holly never waited to confirm plans – as soon as *she* was in, she assumed I would be, too. Until this moment, her assumption had always been correct as I often changed my schedule to see her. But December 21st was the date I'd promised to take C.J. to see Legends on Ice.

A week later, I headed home for winter break, still undecided about what I was going to do. On the night of the show, I asked my dad if he thought C.J. would mind skipping it.

"It feels like you're seeking permission for something you know is wrong," he said.

"Maybe you or Mom could take him."

"Or you could honor your commitment," he replied. "Why on earth are you trying to get out of this? I thought you were looking forward to it."

"Some friends are getting together tonight and I wanted to meet up."

"So see your friends some other time these next two weeks."

I pulled my phone from my pocket.

"Listen, we can dance around this or you can admit there's a girl you want to see. I've been there, but C.J. is your brother. He'll be your brother for the rest of your life and even though he can't always find ways to show it, he loves you."

"What time is Mom coming home from work?"

"Really? Are you joking, because I can't tell from the tone of your voice."

"I'm not joking, Dad."

"Listen Matthew, this is a chance for you to close the gap between the young man that you are and the young man that you want to be. Don't let a moment like this slip by."

The garage door opened, the Subaru Outback door slammed and my mother walked into the kitchen. "Slippery out there," she said. As my mother took off her wool coat, I asked her whether she'd be interested in taking C.J. to Legends on Ice.

My mom looked over at my dad, like two professional musicians at the end of a song silently communicating about the final chords. "I'd love to honey," she said, "but C.J has been anticipating this evening for a long time and I know you have, too."

My brother walked in on the tail end of the conversation. "Here's the person you should be talking to," my mother said, giving C.J. a fist bump. He looked at me. "What are we going to talk about, Matty?"

I looked at my cell phone and scrolled to the photo of Holly holding the sign. "I wanted to talk to you about Legends on Ice," I said.

"Can we get a program?" C.J. asked. "I really want a program so we can see who's in the show." My brother looked at me, waiting for an answer. He eyed my phone. "Do you think anybody will fall down, Matty?"

My face felt hot. "I hope so," I said. C.J. laughed.

"Me, too," he said.

"That seems mean," my mother said.

"It's just that C.J and I like when that happens. He likes it when I fall on the ice."

"Yeah, we like that," my brother repeated.

"I must have been at work when we were supposed to teach you to not laugh at other people's misfortunes," my mother said.

"I think it was the time you and Dad went to Hawaii for the week and left us with a babysitter," I said. The three of them looked at me silently, letting my lame joke hang in the air.

"What time do you two need to be leaving?" my father asked.

More silence. My phone buzzed. I didn't dare look at it. My family waited.

I resented my father for his obvious effort to paint me into a corner. That resentment quickly transformed into a deeper sense of loss as I grieved for all the carefree moments of my adolescence that I had undoubtedly missed out on when I was watching over my brother, including this lost romantic opportunity with Holly.

Outside, a flashing orange light from a snowplow lit up the street. I could hear the salt from the truck as it landed on the icy roads.

"Do you think somebody will fall down, Matty?" my brother asked again.

My mother smiled at me because she knew what was going to happen. "I'm going to freshen up and get ready for dinner," she announced.

"Hey C.J., I've got an idea," I said. How about we grab a bite at Tubby's Burgers before the show?"

My father handed me twenty bucks for dinner. I wandered down to my bedroom, closed the door and reached for my cell. It's been a few years since I made that phone call and to this day, I can remember every single word from the conversation that began with a simple, familiar greeting: "Hey, it's me."

Super Destroyer is Choking His Opponent

(1994)

The knuckles on my Grandma Vi's wrinkled hands whitened as she clenched them into tight fists. She looked ready to take a swing at somebody. Viola, a former elementary school librarian who remained patient and calm even as she tired of reading another Caldecott Medal-winning book to her wiggly students, the woman who spoke four languages and survived a World War II refugee camp, the woman who took up yoga at age 65 and was hired as an instructor at her local YWCA two years later, had become addicted to professional wrestling while dying in a nursing home.

"For God's sake, Super Destroyer is choking his opponent," my grandmother yelled at the television. Her fingers, thin as popsicle sticks, pounded the bed, knocking aside the two large-print *Reader's Digests* and rosary that I'd set there moments earlier. Grandma Vi's extra set of dentures sat on the nightstand next to her bed, a strange reminder of the futility of her obsession with oral health.

My grandmother's state of captivity became inevitable shortly after the death of her husband. Grandpa George's ability to conceal Viola's declining health became clear as soon as he passed away. She got lost as she walked five blocks to her weekly bridge club game. Then she neglected to pay her utility and phone bills. Finally, on a trip home from the grocery store, Grandma Vi plowed her pristine 1969 powder blue Ford Falcon into half a dozen mailboxes and three revered rose bushes, which upset her neighbors more than the fallen soldier mailboxes. A month later, my father placed his mother in Sunset Hills Nursing Home, a world of three narrow hallways, a twin bed, a nightstand, a television, a bulletin board and little else.

My Grandpa George always admired pro wrestling, but even in his final days, he understood that every battle between good and evil was well-scripted. He'd sit in his squeaky recliner with a bag of pork rinds and a can of Pabst, waving off Grandma Vi when she scolded him for watching such trash. Now, as my grandmother sat in her tiny nursing home room, *she* was the one paying close attention to the choreography of the pro wrestlers on television. Even worse, she seemed to believe that their battles were real.

"He's choking him on the rope," she yelled. "Can't anybody else see that?"

"Grandma, why are you watching this crap? It's just a bunch of gymnasts on steroids."

"Crap? Is that the way you young people talk these days?"

I picked up my grandmother's rosary from the dusty tile floor and handed it to her. She twirled the cross around her index finger like a kid wrapping a tetherball around a pole.

I looked at the pictures that our family had pinned to her bulletin board. My eyes locked on a 25-year-old color photo of Viola holding me when I was a toddler. I was nuzzled into my grandmother's neck while she stared out our living room window at snow clinging to the trees, her face revealing the serenity of a woman who knows she's finished raising her own children. Next to that photo was a picture of my Grandma and Grandpa, both holding knives and forks in mock competition as they prepared to carve a golden Thanksgiving turkey.

"Grandma," I said. She looked away from the television and seemed confused by my presence.

"Heavens, how long have you been here, Will?" she asked me.

"I just got here," I lied. "How long have *you* been here?"

"Too long," she replied, squeezing the rosary into her palm. A truck commercial blared from the television, leaving me an opening for the customary question.

"Got any cool stories for me?" I asked.

"Goodness, it's so hard to remember," she said. "My memory leaks like a sieve these days."

Grandma Vi is the family historian, sewing us together with the unbreakable thread of nostalgia. The grandmother I knew until recently could recite, in enthusiastic detail, every important family anecdote from the last 80 years, like the time her life was saved by a snowstorm that covered her muddy footprints when she stole firewood from the guard's supply shed in the World War II refugee camp. Her family stories were fading quickly, more collateral damage of Alzheimer's.

"Tell me about the time Dad stepped in the paint can. I love to hear about Dad getting in trouble."

"Oh, that was so long ago."

"Grandpa George totally scratched the living room wall when he put up the Christmas tree, right? And he was touching up the wall with paint when Dad accidentally stepped in the tray."

"Oh, that's right," she said. "Your grandfather was pretty excitable and this was a pretty exciting thing. When your dad stepped in that paint, George yelled at your father like the house was on fire. It scared the jeepers out of your poor father because he hopped out of that little paint tray and made a beeline for his bedroom."

"Then what happened?" I asked.

"Well, your grandpa dropped his brush and dove headfirst over our coffee table to grab your father before he could make paint marks throughout the house, but your father got away and made a crooked path of tiny white footprints on the carpet all the way to his bedroom. George was furious. I've never seen a grown man so angry. He gave your father a real spanking, more than he ever had before."

In each of her previous renditions of the story, Grandma had never mentioned the punishment. "I guess that explains Dad's fear of latex paint," I said.

"Your grandpa shouldn't have gotten so upset," she said. "It was a child's mistake. Your father couldn't have been more than four or five years old. I only wish that I'd stuck up for him at the time."

I'd never heard Grandma make this admission. Did she always have these thoughts and just lack the nerve to voice them? Or was she settling things in her head as she neared the end of her life?

The television announcer's voice rose with sudden drama, luring my grandmother back to the world of wrestling.

"Look out!" my grandmother yelled as Super Destroyer flew off the top rope onto his foe. "That Super Destroyer is awful, just awful. He cheats and cheats and the referee never does a thing about it."

"You know the rules of professional wrestling?"

"Of course I do."

I laughed. "Grandma, look how short that referee is. What do you expect him to do?"

"All I know is that somebody's going to get hurt." Grandma dangled the rosary from her finger.

"Do you want me to put that away for you?" I asked.

"I've been on this planet for nearly 90 years," she said, her voice rising. "I think I'm capable of hanging on to a rosary."

This slap stunned me more than her new love of bad television. She had never said a harsh word to me. "Grandma, remember how you used to buy those scrawny Christmas trees from your neighbor? And remember how you'd never let any of us kids eat rum balls after Christmas dinner because they had liquor in them?"

The wrestlers commanded her attention. We could be trapped in a cave for all she cared, just as long as it had good television reception. I made a tiny circle with my fingers on her shoulder. She shook her head slightly without looking at me.

"Do you remember any other Christmas stories?" I asked. "Like the time I fainted after I sang that solo at the fourth grade Christmas concert? You tied my tie a little too tight and I collapsed on stage during 'Joy to the World.'"

"He's choking him again," she said. Grandma threw her arms up in disgust and for a minute, I thought she was going to wrap her hands around my neck in a fake choke hold.

"How about the time you took us to the Ice Capades on Christmas Eve and none of us could remember where we'd parked? We thought Santa would skip our house if we didn't get home and get to bed in time."

"Well, that fight's over," she replied. "Why do the rotten apples always win?"

I played along until I could think of a way to coax her back. "So who fights next?" I asked.

"Jerry Springer. He has the damnedest people on that program."

"Grandma, I've never heard you swear."

"Just wait until you're my age and get stuck living with a bunch of old people. You'll swear, too."

"I don't mind," I said. "Sometimes I like to swear."

"At my age, honesty is all I have left."

I walked back to the bulletin board, unpinned the picture of Grandma holding me and placed it in front of her.

She smiled as she looked at the photograph. "Who is that?"

"It's me and you. I think it was taken during one of those Christmas Day snowstorms."

"Beautiful picture, whoever it is."

"I told you, Grandma, that's a picture of you holding me."

"Oh, my goodness. Sometimes I have a hard time remembering, that's all."

"Don't worry about it," I said. I picked up the photograph and tacked it back on to her bulletin board.

I hated watching my grandmother's life become so small. My efforts to distract her with Christmas stories and family pictures suddenly felt naïve. At that moment, as Grandma stared at the television screen, I understood that our common biology, geography and history were not enough to slow the momentum of time. Too often, age turns loved ones into strangers.

"Will?"

"Yeah?"

"I should have stood up for your father when he stepped in the paint," she said. "Please tell him I'm sorry."

Grandma Viola smoothed out the rumpled blanket on her bed. She closed her eyes and gently traced the shape of her rosary with her fingers.

"He'll be here in a couple of days to pick you up for Christmas Eve dinner. You can tell him yourself," I replied. "You know that Dad always likes it when people apologize to him."

My grandma laughed. "When is Christmas Eve?" she asked.

"Three days from today." We both knew it would likely be her last.

The wrinkles on my grandmother's face tightened momentarily as she thought about what to say next. "You like hearing these stories, Will, but you need to know almost everything I learned was built on some mistake or misunderstanding. So it's hard to re-live them all the time."

"It's okay," I said. "I won't ask you again if it's too painful." I got up to leave.

"I know it's fake, Will. The wrestling."

"Of course you do."

"It reminds me of your ridiculous grandfather. That's why I watch it."

"Got it. I miss him, too." When my grandfather died, Grandma Vi kept his cremated remains in a large Ziplock plastic bag on her dining room table until she could decide where to spread his ashes. She said it helped her "keep on eye on him" but I think it was just another way for her to prolong the memory of their time together.

"Your grandfather wasn't a polished man but he was always fair and kind. I still can't believe he left me here alone."

"I'm sure it wasn't his first choice."

Grandma Vi stared at the television as Jerry Springer came on.

"He loved you so much," I said. My grandma didn't say anything. She flicked off the television with her remote control.

"I don't like Super Destroyer," I said. "He's a heel."

"Neither do I," my grandmother replied. "He shouldn't be allowed to win." My grandmother pivoted her legs so they hung off the side of the bed and asked me to help her get in her wheelchair. I pushed her to the other side of the room so she could look out the window.

"Should I bring pork rinds tomorrow? Real wrestling fans eat pork rinds, you know."

She didn't answer me, lost momentarily as she gazed out at the dimming daylight over the nursing home parking lot.

What It Feels Like

(2004)

—◆—

As I approached the ferry dock, I expected to see a long line of people who wanted to witness a miracle, but there were only two of us.

The other passenger wore a puffy black North Face jacket, camouflage cargo pants, a baseball cap discolored with sweat stains and a thin moustache that resembled two black Allen wrenches. He carried a lumpy Army duffel bag with "Ernesto Lozano" stenciled along the side.

The small water taxi pulled up to the dock and let off a handful of departing passengers. The captain, who looked more like an aging roofer than a boat skipper in his old flannel shirt, dirty blue jeans and steel-toed work boots, took our tickets and introduced himself as Paul. We stepped inside the cabin for a brief passage across the middle tentacle of southern Puget Sound.

"Looks like you fellas are it for tonight," Paul said. He glanced at the empty pier to make sure there were no other passengers. "What brings you to Anderson Island?"

Ernesto stayed silent. "I'm a writer," I said.

A.J., my old college roommate, worked as an assistant editor at *Esquire*. He knew I'd hit a rough patch so he had invited me to submit an article for "What It Feels Like," a feature in which people describe extraordinary events they've experienced, like being struck by lightning or attacked by a tiger or undergoing a sex change operation. For the article, I needed to find an eyewitness to tell me what it felt like to experience a miracle. A.J. promised that if the story was good enough, he'd get it into the magazine.

"You're heading for St. Mike's then," Paul said. As he turned to look at us, I admired his weather-beaten face with its deep lines around his eyes and forehead, like tributaries that shifted direction when he spoke or smiled.

"Lucky guess," I replied. The Catholic church on Anderson Island was home to a statue of the Virgin Mary that wept blood recently. Despite the fact that the trip took me away from my wife and two kids during the weekend before Christmas, I felt the usual thrill of hunting down a good story. Plus, I needed the money.

"You'll be disappointed," Paul said.

"Why would you say that?" I asked, half-amused, half-irritated. I'd always been fascinated by the intersection of paranormal phenomenon and religious faith -- weeping statues, a bleeding crown of thorns, oil emerging from spiritual icons -- all of these mysteries intrigued me, regardless of the explanations of professional debunkers.

"First of all, Mary's not crying any more," Paul said.

"When did she stop?" I asked.

"Month or so ago. Right around Thanksgiving."

A cell phone rang. Ernesto dug around his duffel bag and found it after three rings. "Hello." Fifteen seconds of listening. "Yes, I told you I'd do this." More listening. "You don't mean that."

The cabin seemed to shrink and even though the skipper revved the engine a bit higher to give Ernesto some privacy, it wasn't enough.

Ernesto massaged his forehead with his left hand. "A few days. As soon as I can. No, I can't." More silence. "That's not a good idea." He exhaled. "Give them a hug for me. No, don't worry about that."

Ernesto put the phone in his duffel bag and said something in Spanish that had the bitterness of a curse. I am ashamed to admit that I took solace in overhearing his conversation. The evident conflict in Ernesto's life made me feel less lonely.

I looked over at him and tried desperately to keep my mouth shut as the dark waters of Puget Sound gently rolled the boat back and forth. Over the years, I had battled addictions to stories of personal hardship as well as the excessive drinking that often seemed to accompany the pursuit of those stories.

The breaking point revealed itself when my friend Andrew and I raced over to his girlfriend's house as she was on the verge of suicide and I thought only about how I might find a way to write about the experience, regardless of the outcome. That night, after we found my buddy's girlfriend safe, I drank until I passed out at our kitchen table. In the morning, my wife told me that I'd had enough liquor to last me for the next three presidential administrations and said it needed to end. Since then, I'd been on the wagon for 139 days and I had not written anything more compelling than a shopping list. Ernesto's conversation was too much. Simple human decency compelled an inquiry.

"Everything okay?"

He stared out the window. "You ever been married?"

"Ten years' worth."

He didn't respond for a few minutes. Silence, a reporter's best weapon, took over.

"It's too hard," he said finally. "My wife. She's so religious. I'm not sure when it happened."

"What's wrong with that?" I asked.

"It's too much. Bible study groups. Church meetings. Private school for our kids. Evening prayers. All of it."

"Maybe she's trying to protect them in a way that she understands."

"She says things under her breath. One time I swore in front of the girls and my wife said, 'Did you hear that, Lord?' Or when I ask her to do something she'll whisper, 'Dios, dame paciencia.'" Ernesto cracked his knuckles. "God, give me patience."

"I thought my mom was the only person who said that," I replied.

The lights of the ferry terminal at Anderson Island appeared as tiny dots across the Sound. Paul turned the boat directly into the waves and the water thumped lightly against the hull. "She sent me here. My wife. She says if I love her, I needed to come see the weeping Virgin Mary. She thinks it will help me come back to Jesus. I think she wants me to miss Christmas."

"That's rough."

"Last week she told the kids that she is going to put up a sign telling Santa not to stop at our house this year. She says we already have enough toys and Santa should save them for less fortunate kids."

"No Santa? I can't imagine how my two boys would react to something like that," I said. "How old are your kids?"

"Teresita's seven and Maria's five. They're sweet girls, you know? But it's getting harder for them. The constant pressure."

Paul looked up from a log book where he had written something. "I know I'm just buttin' in, but your wife's right," he said. "With all the garbage going on these days, everybody forgets the damn point of Christmas. Non-stop shopping and for what? A pizza cooker? Dancing Santas for the front lawn?" He shook his head. Ernesto looked at me and didn't say anything which seemed to embolden the captain.

"If you ask me, this country is filled with trash. Girls dressing like hookers. Boys with their britches hanging so low their ass shows when they walk. Filthy music. Your wife is right. You should thank her and get with the program."

"I've tried. I go to church. I pray. I drove four hours to come here," he said, motioning toward the island.

I wondered whether Ernesto's marriage would survive his reluctant faith.

"Let's face it," Paul said, "there are two big forces in our society -- God and pop culture. One of them is gaining power and one is losing. This weeping Madonna is all pop culture. Hell, Father Riley wanted to move the statue to the church basement when all this began but the President of the local Chamber of Commerce begged him to wait until after Christmas. That's how the world really works."

Paul turned on the wipers as the sea spray swirled into the boat's windshield.

"So, you think we'll be disappointed when we see the statue?" I asked.

"Listen, son. I'm the only miracle you're going to see tonight. The ferry company cut back the water taxi runs to Anderson and laid me off until all you lookie-loos started coming here. I got my job back. That's a miracle. I've been married for 37 years. You gentlemen know that's a miracle! I've beaten cancer twice. I am one defunct outfit. It's a miracle I'm still above ground."

"So, you've seen the Virgin Mary already?" Ernesto asked.

"Course I have."

"And?"

"And what? You think God needs to resort to parlor tricks like weeping statues? You mainlanders are something else. Only time we see you in church is when somebody's playing a hoax."

"But there are lots of examples throughout history of this happening," I said. "There are eyewitnesses."

"Listen, I've read all about how easy it is to jury-rig a crying statue and if a dim bulb like me can figure it out..."

"You think somebody on the island created a hoax?" I asked.

"Of course not! Folks here are too salt-of-the-earth for that kind of nonsense."

"Then how do you explain it?"

"Hell, I don't know, probably a leaky pipe somewhere."

"That would be pretty easy to spot."

"I knew this was a waste of time," Ernesto said. He stared out the window, resignation overwhelming exhaustion.

"Listen, people come to this island with all sorts of crazy ideas so who knows how it got started. Don't worry, I'll drive you over to the church. It's half a mile from my house and I'm done for the night. You can check it out and I'll drop you wherever you're staying on my way home." Paul scratched his head and shifted a pack of cigarettes from his back pants pocket to his front shirt pocket.

"Wait until you see our living nativity scene," Paul said. "Forget about the weeping Madonna. You want to see a sign? Check out the happy faces of these kids who stand in the cold wind and rain until their fingers fall off from frostbite."

Paul deftly glided the boat up to the dock, hopped out and tied a bow line and stern line to the iron cleats. Within minutes, he'd locked up the ferry and we piled into his Ford Bronco. As we drove, I wondered if the power was out on the island because there were so few lights on along the way. He pulled up to the gravel parking lot of a tiny church and steered the Bronco into a handicapped spot. "We're here."

The three of us walked together toward the nativity scene. Under a cluster of Douglas fir trees near the entrance of the church, a dozen children and twice as many adults huddled around a makeshift plywood manger. A combination of temporary floodlights and car lights illuminated the scene.

The children in the nativity seemed content to spend a Saturday night creating this living postcard. A pair of girls, dressed as angels, looked serenely at a bundled up baby doll in the crib. Three shepherds in mismatching headdresses, bulky gowns and rudimentary staffs kept watch. Pre-adolescent versions of Joseph and Mary looked down at the manger, hands clasped in prayer. The participants were remarkably quiet, save the occasional rustling of shoes as they fidgeted to keep warm. One of the shepherds stood up on a hay bale and broke the silence. "Hail Mary, full of grace." A phalanx of phones recorded the moment.

As the children in their homemade costumes recited the prayer, their collective breaths emitted tiny clouds into the damp night. One of the angels smiled at us. Despite the solemnity of these children, their hope, their devotion, I couldn't resist the pull of the mystery inside the church. I walked to the front door. The other two followed.

"Over there," Paul said, pointing to an alcove in the back right corner lit only by candles. Ernesto and I stood side by side in front of the statue. I stared at the Virgin Mary, noting her fading paint for what seemed like a long time. Along her left eye running down to her left cheek was a trail of deep red. I wondered when and if workers at the church would clean the line of blood from the statue. I shifted to the side to look at Mary from a different angle, shamelessly using the light from my cell phone to brighten her face so I could see if anything looked suspicious. My eyes grew dry and I held them shut for a minute, waiting to see what images emerged.

When I opened them, I felt the moment sneak up on me. Like my fellow passenger, I wanted to find something here, something more than a story. I wanted the statue to revive my dormant faith, heal my addictions and help carry me through the tenuous moments in my own life.

Time passed. I waited. I looked up again at the Virgin Mary, overwhelmed by the quiet. Outside, one of the children recited the beautiful passage from Luke, Chapter 2: "But the angel said, 'do not be afraid. I bring you news of great joy to be shared by the whole people.'"

I glanced over at Ernesto. His eyes, tired, locked on the statue and his expression shifted subtly from fatigue to curiosity to contentment. After several minutes, he closed his eyes, made the sign of the cross and whispered, "gracias por amarme." He walked down the center aisle of the church and kneeled down in a pew. Outside, the children began to sing, "Away in a Manger" in surprisingly good pitch. I kneeled down next to Ernesto and waited for the singing to end.

Paul walked towards us and I motioned him away. I watched as he sauntered to the other side of the church, pulled a cigarette from a crushed pack, put it in his mouth and leaned down by one of the glowing remembrance candles to light it. "I'll be out at the nativity scene," he said. "You fellas take as long as you need."

Ernesto bowed his head. "Our Father, who art in heaven, hallowed be thy name." I prayed along silently and waited for him to finish. When he was done, he let out a deep breath. "You're a writer. Did you experience anything?" Ernesto asked me.

My neck started to itch in the dry heat of the church. "I didn't feel a thing," I said. "I wanted to. I prayed for my marriage, for my kids, for help with my problems. But it mostly made me feel more alone."

"I'm sorry," he said. He looked over at the statue of the Virgin Mary.

"How about you?" I asked.

"I had an epiphany," he said. "Something happened."

"Can you tell me about it?"

A priest walked out from a room off of the altar and headed over to us. "I'm sorry, the church is closing for the night," he said.

Ernesto and I walked toward the parking lot. Outside the children sang "Silent Night" as a final act of the living nativity.

"Where do you think we can get a beer on this island?" he asked.

I had been on the wagon for four months and feared what might happen if we went out. I had gotten back on the right side of my wife and children in recent months. But the promise of hearing Ernesto's story, his full story, paralyzed me.

"What did it feel like?" I asked.

"You won't believe me," he said. He smiled as we walked past the children gathered with their parents and the three church volunteers who were taking down the lights from the living nativity scene.

90 Degrees North[*]

(2011)

———•✦•———

As the Wright family returned from Christmas Eve mass (the late afternoon service featuring a joyless youth choir and their proud parents clutching cameras rather than hymnals) Amanda pointed out a box sitting underneath the Christmas tree. "Hey, what's that over there?" she asked.

A few hours earlier Amanda had secretly placed the present, a hastily wrapped Nerf gun, under the tree. Ever since her Chess Club colleagues had convinced Amanda that Santa was not real, she had taken it upon herself to prop up the rickety faith of her older brother, Elijah, who had somehow managed to sustain his belief in the magic of the old man. Amanda hoped to fool her older brother into believing that while they were singing "O Come All Ye Faithful" at St. James Catholic Church, Santa had executed a pre-emptive gift drop.

Elijah looked at his sister funny and turned to his parents. "Can I open it?"

"It seems early to get started," his father said, "but if Santa decided to leave you an extra present, you should go ahead and open it." He turned to his wife. "If Amanda had really been hoping to trick Elijah,

_____

[*] *This story contains spoilers about the magic of Christmas and Santa. The content may not be suitable for younger readers.*

she should have complained about why there was no present *for her* under the tree. That would have been much more convincing."

Within minutes, Elijah had unfurled the weapon, filled its chambers with a dozen orange foam bullets and strafed various living room targets: a pile of Cheetos left on a plate, a WWE wrestling figure, the tail of their cat, Rocco, and the carefully arranged ceramic manger scene sitting on top of the coffee table.

"Sorry. That was an accident," Elijah said immediately, sensing an impending punishment. He quickly placed the Three Wise Men back onto their designated spots and returned Baby Jesus onto his back in the manger.

"It had damned well better be," warned his mother.

"Who was this present from again?" he asked.

"Santa?" asked Amanda.

"Yeah, right," Elijah replied. "First of all, Santa doesn't deliver in the middle of the afternoon. He's not the UPS man. Second, where is *your* present?" Amanda shrugged.

●✦●

As the Wright children hustled down the stairs on Christmas morning, their parents shook off their sleep-deprivation fog. The soundtrack never varied: loud paper ripping, joyful yelling and screaming, consternation over how to slice through industrial-strength plastic toy packaging, expressions of appreciation. This time, however, those sounds were interrupted by a brief silence as the two siblings spotted an envelope amongst the packages. Amanda opened it to find a customized note along with a photograph of Santa standing next to their Christmas tree. Amanda read it out loud. Her face scrunched as she tried to figure out what she knew, what she thought she knew and what she was no longer certain about. Elijah kept up his usual

Christmas morning patter, equal parts wonder, obsession and enthusiasm, his faith confirmed. Amanda and her mother pondered the possibility of a Christmas miracle.

Mrs. Wright ran her thumb across the picture of Santa several times, like a spy checking to see if the ink was somehow still wet. "Is that you?" she asked her husband quietly.

He scowled. "I think that guy has about 40 pounds and 30 years on me but thanks for the compliment."

•✦•

Excerpt from Martha Stewart magazine, Holiday Issue, 10 Questions For... Christopher Worthy

This month, *10 Questions For...* features Christopher Worthy, the 32-year-old founder and CEO of one of the most surreptitious companies in Washington State, 90 Degrees North. Although Worthy refused to be photographed for this article, he did reveal several details about his thriving business.

MS: How does 90 Degrees North work exactly? You don't advertise, is that right?

CW: That's right. Ninety Degrees North has no web presence and does no advertising. We operate solely by word-of-mouth. Confidentiality is key to keeping the magic alive so we meet personally with each customer. The best clients don't tell their spouses or partners about our services because that makes it even more enchanting. Our company sends Santa surrogates directly into homes to deliver Christmas presents when our clients are sleeping or away.

MS: How do you do it?

CW: Rule number one is never get caught. We've gotten very good at getting in and out of houses quickly and quietly. Ideally, we come in when families are away for part of the night and then we deliver wrapped presents along with a personalized, hand-written note to the recipients from Santa.

MS: Is that enough to convince the doubters?

CW: Sometimes. But the coup de grace is the picture of Santa holding the boxes of gifts inside the house. We leave the note and Polaroid photo next to the presents because for many of us, seeing is believing, especially if it's a picture of Santa inside your home. About the only thing our Santas don't do is climb down the chimney.

MS: How did your company get its start?

CW: I remembered how difficult it had been for my parents to let go of Santa and it inspired me to start 90 Degrees North. You'd think it would be hard on the kids, but sometimes it's tougher on the parents. My folks arranged for a letter postmarked from the North Pole and tried all sorts of tricks to keep the thrill alive. That always stuck with me. After college, I worked briefly as a house cleaner and one of my customers asked if I could put Christmas presents out before I left. I launched the company the following year.

MS: Who were your first customers?

CW: When 90 Degrees North started out, we were a boutique service firm. Most of our customers were affluent families. A couple of these families had extensive security systems, so it was fun for them to check their video footage and see moving images of Santa in their home. More recently, clients have hired us to provide gifts to aging parents and other people who might be inspired by a dose of Christmas spirit. We've had at least a dozen jobs for people who are suffering from a terminal illness. Their loved ones want to provide one more opportunity to experience the wonder and mystery of Christmas. I can't think of a nicer gift.

MS: Do you think your customers are looking to create an experience that defies our technology-driven culture?

CW: Clearly our service strikes a chord for a lot of people who have nostalgia for an old-fashioned Christmas. Let's face it, kids can Google all kinds of information about Santa. Sometimes you have to create a bit of magic to combat that.

As the Wright boys finished their gift opening exercise, Amanda hauled a box over to the couch where her mother and father were perched. "I got a chess set and it wasn't something I asked for but I really need it because I lost four pawns, so I always have to use the ugly plastic guys from Candyland," she said. "I'm happy Santa brought that for me."

"Yeah, that's a great surprise," his mother said. When Amanda turned away, she whispered to her husband. "Good job on that one." Her husband smiled weakly, knowing that he had not included the chess set on the wish list he submitted to 90 Degrees North.

Excerpt from Martha Stewart magazine, Holiday Issue, 10 Questions For…Christopher Worthy

MS: So, as I understand it, customers of 90 Degrees North provide the names and ages of the recipient and a specific shopping list. The company does all the rest?

CW: We take all of the hassle out of Christmas. We do all the shopping, the wrapping, you name it.

MS: What kinds of feedback do you receive from your customers?

CW: They love our service mostly because it's so magical. There is a surprise for everybody. I developed an algorithm that analyzes the presents on the wish list, identifies another item the recipient might like and adds it to the order. The extra present is always wrapped separately. It adds to the mystery – including for the person who hired us. We get a ton of phone calls right after Christmas but we deny everything.

• ◆ •

After breakfast as Amanda and Elijah played with their new toys, a Nerf gun dart landed at the backside of the tree, just missing an expensive glass ornament. As she retrieved the bullet, Amanda spied one more present partially hidden underneath the tree skirt. It was wrapped in a newspaper with a foreign language that she did not recognize. She pulled it out and brought it over to her brother. "This one doesn't have any name tag on it," Amanda said. Elijah stared at the newspaper. "I can't read this. Let's rip it open."

Amanda carefully unwrapped the present, a brightly painted wooden doll. "What's this thing?" she said handing it to her father. Mr. Wright turned a Russian nesting doll in his hand. The crow's feet wrinkles around his eyes deepened as he inspected the toy and then eased as he smiled. The father handed it to Elijah. "Open it up," he said.

"Open what up?" he asked. Elijah held the toy soldier at arm's length as if it might explode. His father took it and pulled the wooden soldier apart to reveal a smaller wooden boy. Elijah twisted the smaller doll at the stomach revealing another boy and the process continued with several iterations, each one eliciting another round of belly laughs.

"They look like they were all carved from the same piece of wood," remarked their father as he carefully turned each of the toys in his hands. "Beautiful." He picked up the discarded wrapping paper and examined the Russian newspaper. "Those guys are good," he said to himself.

• ◆ •

Excerpt from Martha Stewart magazine, Holiday Issue, 10 Questions For…Christopher Worthy

MS: What's been the biggest surprise as you've watched your company grow?

CW: I know this is going to be hard to believe but last year, we got half a dozen calls from various customers who had received Russian nesting dolls as one of their Christmas presents. I love them but it's not exactly the kind of thing our Santas leave for kids. Those dolls are practically extinct as far as I can tell. Hell, I don't even know where I would find a supplier that makes them anymore. It's a lost art.

MS: You had half a dozen customers who all received Russian nesting dolls, but you didn't deliver them?

CW: Swear to God. I told my staff; it sounds like somebody was conning the con man. We checked our records to see if any of these customers had a video security system so we could look at the surveillance footage but none of them did. I'm still trying to figure it out.

●✦●

Amanda and Elijah Wright sauntered into the living room to give their parents a hug good night. As they did so, their father noticed a framed photograph with a tiny red bow sitting on top of the coffee table next to the manger scene. He walked over to it, picked it up and showed it to his wife. The two children and their parents were standing on what looked like the top of a bluff, lit perfectly by the glow of a fading sunset. Each of the Wright family members appeared to be on the verge of hearing a punch line to a very funny joke.

"Where is this from?" asked Amanda.

"I have no idea," said her mother. "I don't even know when it was taken."

"I've never seen this photo before," said her father. "It's got to be the best one ever taken of the four of us."

"Yeah, that is good," said Elijah as he quickly glanced at the picture. He smiled as he walked upstairs to go to bed.

About the Author

Peter Rex is a writer whose work has appeared in The Chicago Tribune, Pacific Northwest Magazine, Oregon Coast Magazine and other publications. He lives in Olympia, Washington with his wife, Ann. This is his first collection of short stories.